AF358489

The Night of Destiny

Lali Dexeus

Translated by Elie Kerrigan

The Night of Destiny

Editing: www.triunfacontulibro.com

ISBN: 9 788409435142

www.lalidexeus.es

ÍNDEX

To my son, Kilian

CHAPTER 1

UPPER AMPURDÁN, 1973

Marco slammed the car door shut. Sighing, he looked around, then strode toward the farmhouse. The burden of difficulties between him and Aline and the short amount of time that he had to unload the drug hidden in his yacht—the Saudade—overwhelmed him. He had the feeling that the accumulated tension of the past couple of days, coupled with his natural aggressiveness, would bring about more problems than usual. He always took things with an inordinate amount of sarcasm, lying to himself because he wished to believe that his wife would understand him. But he was well aware that no matter how hard he tried to explain to her the white powder's profits, she'd never accept it.

As he moved along the cypress-lined path, taking in the warm breeze that rose from the sea, he saw her in the distance. It was that hour of the evening when it is neither day nor night, that hour in which his wife was in the habit of going for a walk. He approached with the intention of having a word with her, but she just stood there, arms crossed behind her back and her head slightly tilted toward the ground as if engaged in a conversation with her own thoughts. He put his arm across her shoulder whilst he accompanied her in silence to the old farmhouse. There and then, he decided that he didn't want to lose her for anything in the world, but it was impossible for him to give in to the temptation of abandoning his commitments, for it meant endangering their lives, even though Aline could hardly suspect it.

As soon as they reached the dining room, Marco, still standing, poured himself a glass of whiskey. Since it was time for some explanations, he observed her, thinking how much she puzzled him even though he thought he knew her well.

She seemed calm in spite of the circumstances. Her sharp face and perfect features, small, in harmony with her slender body, gave her an image of fragility, but deep down, his wife was a rock that no hurricane could topple.

"How do you manage to keep calm?" he asked, somewhat bemused.

"I want to know what's going to happen from now on," she answered, ignoring his question and drowning the fear she had endured since the unexpected discovery of the valuable merchandise.

She had suspected her husband's dealings for some time now but was not aware of the extent they could influence her own life.

"Don't worry. Stay put and don't move till I call you in a couple of days," Marco replied impatiently.

For a split second, he realized how unconvincing his words were but lacked the strength to clarify why he was involved in an international drug trafficking ring.

Without further ado, he downed his drink and headed for his room. Aline knew full well that when Marco behaved in this manner, it was best to let him be, but uneasy, he began to pace the room back and forth. She was furious to be caught up in a trap she didn't know how to extricate herself from; till it occurred to her to open the dresser drawer and grab a key. She went out into the garden and down the cypress-lined path in the direction of the little stone house that her father had converted into an office.

Once there, she introduced the key into the lock with difficulty and, with a good push, managed to open the door. As in the past, she'd come up with the ludicrous idea of finding her father and his advice, but he was no longer there to help her. She felt alone and unable to trust anyone. The Meifrén and Grau Sala, affixed to the walls, stood out, making his absence all the more poignant when it was most needed. She harbored the idea that his death was the unfairest thing that had ever happened to her.

Deep in thought, she pictured his aquiline and serene profile, the silver-gray hair, and the sad look on his face during the last months of his life. With this vision in her mind, she sank down on the old sofa, where the two of them had had so many conversations. Everything was as it had been on their last day.

She had been happy with Marco at the farmhouse, always in a special kind of way. She felt as if she were a different person, although only three years had elapsed since their first encounter. To reminisce about it with its consequences was painful now, but she couldn't help that it sprung to mind. She recalled how the initial attraction that had brought them together weakened, giving way in a short time to a restlessness that oppressed her with the same doggedness as her current situation.

They met one August day. She had gone out rowing to get away from the problems that arose after her father's death. She was not afraid of that sea, for she had known it since childhood, despite the fact that her fishermen friends always warned her that it could be treacherous. She was alone in the rowboat; she lay face down and fell asleep. The boat's blows, hitting against the rocks, startled her. On awaking, she saw the waves getting choppier. She tried to sit up, but the rowboat lurched, threatening to capsize.

Suddenly the prow of a yacht appeared behind the cliff, with some sailors moving on deck with the aplomb of those who are in control of the situation. That vision seemed like a miracle, and before she could recover from her astonishment, a voice was yelling at her not to move. She waited anxiously, shaking, till some men jumped from the deck into a motorized lifeboat and, unhitching the ropes, headed toward her. She was thrown a line which she tied to the bow of her rowboat and was slowly towed to the yacht, from where they hung a ladder, while one of them held out his hand to keep her from falling. She held on tight and climbed up with the feeling of leaving a nightmare behind. She was in front of a man in his forties, with a pleasant and seductive appearance, who did not let go or take his eyes off her.

Dripping, she only thought of asking for a towel. The owner of the boat handed it to her, and Aline, whilst making a gesture to grab it, realized her hand was still held between his.

"My name is Marco," he said in English, without suspecting her nationality.

"I don't know what would've happened if you hadn't shown up…My name is Aline," she answered in the same language while covering herself with the towel on realizing that the cold was seeping into her bones.

Marco returned to the helm. She sensed his power of attraction and sat beside him. Little by little, she perked up and started talking to him.

¿Where are you coming from?

"I live in Italy most of the year," he answered. He then shouted a few phrases in Italian to the rest of the crew, who were preparing the anchors at the boat's prow.

"But you speak very good English. No one could tell that you're Italian," she continued inquiringly.

"I've lived in America for many years," he said, looking away. And, without letting go of the rudder, he asked her to take some ropes to his crew. Aline sensed that he was looking for an excuse not to talk about himself anymore.

They sailed to the harbor's entrance. When it was time to moor, she stayed behind with the sailors, feeling a growing attraction toward the Italian's personality. It began to drizzle, and the mugginess presaged a summer storm. He offered her a coffee and suggested that they shelter below deck; she accepted because she figured it was a good opportunity to get to know him better. For a long while, they told of each other's seafaring experiences, for they shared a common passion for the sea.

When the north wind threatened with its arrival, Aline told him that she was returning to the farmhouse. Marco invited her to sail on the Saudade the following day.

"I'll wait for you here," he said, satisfied and sure of having achieved his objective.

"See you tomorrow," she replied and thought how was it possible that, without knowing him, she'd accepted.

No sooner had she stepped on dry land than she headed toward the shack where the fishermen got together. They were happy to see her, as they'd dealt with her ever since she was a child and invited her to a drink. It was not hard for her to get their opinion regarding the Foreigner, the nickname by which Marco was known, for he came across as a mysterious person.

Between drinks, they told her many stories, and it wasn't long before she drew her own conclusions. He was clearly an enigmatic man. He seemed to have lots of money, judging by his boat and the lavish tips he handed out. He drove an ostentatious car, and his calls to all corners of the world from the port's telephone office were talked about, given their frequency.

She hadn't asked him anything about his life but now realized it made no difference. She didn't need to know anything about him; she much preferred to ignore his background because that anonymity gave her the freedom to imagine him in the manner that best suited her.

During the following days, every morning, as if it were an established custom, she'd go down to the port to their rendezvous, which she didn't even arrange beforehand. They'd set sail in search of deserted beaches, fleeing from people and letting the day pass without any sort of responsibility.

Given the number of hours they spent together, Aline could tell that he desired her, although, at times, he seemed to distance himself or even ignore her. But when he first made love to her, he caught her off guard, and she didn't know how to react. Marco could only do it brutally, and she, not knowing why, liked it. Later, while she was showering in the cabin, the Foreigner's confident voice reached her ears through the water curtain, announcing that they would be married, as if it were something she could not refuse.

Coming out of the bathroom, she saw him lying idly on the bunk. She told herself that if she delayed an answer or expressed any doubts, she would lose him forever. Although she thought she was in love, something within her rebelled, confusing her. She did not know what to do. She was twenty, and he was twice her age. Could she face the consequences of a failure? What if this man turned out to be different from what he appeared to be? However, the need to feel loved and protected after the void left by her father's death outweighed the unpredictable future that he offered her. Reality imposed itself in an overwhelming fashion, and she would ultimately decide on her life's path, just as Marco had just finished doing.

"Do you agree?"

"About what?"

"In marrying me."

"Why do you want us to get married?" she asked, sensing how useless it would be to try to find out what prompted him to make such a wish when they hardly knew each other.

He declared succinctly,

"Because." He knew how to seduce her, especially when she expected his approval.

"Yes or no?" he insisted.

Aline felt that she was being invited to play a game of poker and, in spite of sensing the risk, accepted what fate offered.

Marco slept soundly all night. She remained awake until dawn, waiting for a sign, any clue that would help her see her future more clearly. But the cabin's silence was not disrupted by any sound.

She looked out the hatch. The sea, smooth and calm, appeared lake-like. She recalled her friend Doris, who always said: "Lakes calm one down." She finally fell asleep.

Aline finally snapped out of her daydreaming, got up, and closed the door of the stone house as she left, as if the place were a box where she kept her memories. She knew that it was best not to contradict her husband when he was nervous, although she couldn't resign herself to accepting the risky life he led or admit to his dealings.

As she advanced along the cypress-lined path, she saw Marco trying to avoid her as he was preparing to leave. She called out at him, but fearing that she wanted to hold him back, he pressed the car's accelerator and disappeared. He couldn't put off giving orders to his men to transfer the Saudade's cache to the ship that would take it to its destination. He never traveled with merchandise, and, by chance, Aline caught him the first time around. Although it was a timely and smooth operation, it ended up shattering what was left of their marriage.

That sudden absence plunged her into a despondency that prevented her from properly analyzing how best to accept the facts. She realized that she had never been in love with him, even if she had needed him at first. She walked toward the old farmhouse and felt the afternoon's clammy humidity. Pensive, she went up to her bedroom, recalling her childhood's happy and peaceful summers in spite of her parents' disagreements. How could she have guessed that she'd end up living in this manner? A terrible anxiety took hold of her, and she felt a knot in the pit of her stomach. She tried to reflect. The amount of white powder hidden in the Saudade was enough to end up behind bars for a long time.

A few hours later, assuming that Marco must have set sail, she got ready to go down to the port and have a chat with the sailors. Perhaps she'd be able to elicit some information from them that could help her figure out the yacht's destination.

With a firm step, she crossed the parlor and went through the porch. She then drove to the port and parked. As she headed toward the pontoons, a powerful voice made her shudder. She was reassured on seeing that it was José the Fisherman. A strong and taciturn man, but frank and dreamy. As a child, she used to go out fishing with him and her father, and while they waited impatiently for some fish to take the bait, he'd tell them seafaring stories that father and daughter listened to with great interest.

"Your husband set sail a while ago. Is this what you wanted to know?" José said, tapping the sole of his shoe with his pipe, from which singed tobacco spilled.

She looked at the horizon pensively and nodded.

"Where do you think they're headed?"

"They've taken a southwesterly course, so they're probably on their way to the Balearic Islands, or they'll follow the coast toward the south. However, I'm more inclined to believe the former," he answered, pulling out fresh tobacco and lighting the pipe, unable to put into words exactly what he felt.

He knew her well enough to know that, in spite of the obstacles, she would not back down from her intentions. Aline's innate way of being could always count on her father's unconditional support, who never deterred her in the face of any sort of danger. From steering the large boat to sailing on stormy nights, together they faced numerous difficulties, which José witnessed many a time. He never understood this attitude of Henry Asher, Aline's father, toward the girl, but neither he nor anyone in the village dared judge him because they all knew how much he loved her.

He realized that she was still engrossed in her preoccupations, which would be hard for him to understand, but he would help her whichever way he could. So, he asked her to accompany him to the seaside tavern, which was his favorite.

Sitting before the bar's counter, taciturn, he savored an anisette. Beside him, Aline, with a worried countenance, reflected. She did not question the Fisherman's indications, for she was aware of her husband's trips to Ibiza. She then considered the possibilities that he would put in at that island.

The place came back to mind as she recalled the one time that they'd sailed together on its crystalline waters. Unexpectedly, one night, Marco had gone ashore, and the crew, thinking that she had gone with him and certain of her absence, began to drink and make comments out loud that Aline, inadvertently and despite the commotion, overheard. They mentioned a bar called Blue Moon in Dalt Vila, the city's old quarter, and the fellow who ran it, Sonny, a mulatto whose true identity no one knew.

However, from the sailors' gossip, she realized that they were aware of his affairs. It appeared that people from all walks of life and nationalities, either living on the island or in passing, met at this joint: Artists, politicians, millionaires, and hippies mingled, soused on Sonny's explosive cocktails and seeking the white powder that he provided them with. The mulatto, it turned out, possessed an extraordinary memory and could remember the secrets that his faithful clients entrusted to him for years so that at some point in the future and at the right moment, he would sell them to the highest bidder.

Aline, at the time, didn't give this gossip much importance, but given what had occurred, she realized that it could come in handy. It now occurred to her that if Marco was on the island, Sonny would know his whereabouts. Ibiza was too small to shelter, without their relating, two characters involved in the drug world.

Broken voices singing melodious habaneras brought her back to the present.

"Did you say 'to the Balearic Islands most likely?'"

José, who had fallen silent in front of the half-empty bottle, confirmed it.

Aline took a deep breath. The night seemed endless. Tired, she said goodbye to the Fisherman, who only managed to show his concern by saying, "Be careful!"

But she no longer heard him. She parted from his company as quickly as she wished to dispel the present from her life.

Outside the joint, she paused a few seconds, overwhelmed by the crashing waves. She thought he hadn't picked the right night to sail, though she could swear he had no choice. She felt helpless, like the waves that inevitably ended up on shore, and again went back to her refuge.

CHAPTER 2

IBIZA, 1973

A couple of days later, she was on a flight headed for the island. No sooner had she stepped off the plane than a sweltering heat and a looming fear greeted her. It was as if a storm about to burst incited the atmosphere to the point of suffocation. She crossed the airport terminal, angry at herself for being in such a real and dramatic situation. But once seated in the taxi, the aggravation that she'd been at pains to keep under control began to subside as she recalled the adverse circumstances that her father had lived through and the courage with which he dealt with them. She told herself that she must be strong and face reality.

The afternoon wore on. She sat back on a wicker chair on the terrace of the bar next to the Blue Moon and waited impatiently for the mulatto, realizing how upset Marco would be if she were to discover his whereabouts. As for the Saudade, as expected, there was no trace of it in the port.

She was musing how best to reorganize the future when, suddenly, her train of thought was interrupted on seeing a short, dark-skinned man descending the slope, sporting strange tattoos on his chest and hiding part of his face under a visor. She guessed that it was the fellow she was looking for as he entered the Blue Moon. Puzzled, she realized that it would be best to have no dealings whatsoever with him, but something inside her egged her on.

She allowed for a few minutes to go by before heading toward the premises. Once inside, she had the impression of being in a cocktail bar in Papeete, given the exotic decoration and the soft background music typical of the South Seas.

Sonny, behind the bar, looked up, gave her a quick glance, and carrying on counting a stack of bills, asked in a rude tone, "What do you want?"

"Do you know Marco Partana, an Italian who often comes with his boat, the Saudade?" She ventured to ask without beating around the bush.

"Who are you?"

"Tell him that it's Aline and that I'm here," she replied, feigning that she knew much more of what was only a supposition.

Taken aback, the mulatto pushed the wad aside, fixed his attention on her for a split second, and then with a somewhat calculated slowness, reached for the visor and, with a cracked smile, said, "Wait."

Aline, without taking her eyes off him, watched through the windows as he headed for the phone booth a few steps from the bar. The conversation that Sonny had with the invisible interlocutor was brief, for he was back in the blink of an eye. From the doorway, he beckoned at her to come closer, and when she was in front of him, he said tersely, "I'll drive you to the Italian's place."

Without further ado, he took one of the many keys hanging from his belt, locked the premises, and headed down a narrow, steep alley that led to the old church.

She briefly doubted the veracity of his words but had no choice. She assumed the risk and followed him to the little square, where it was made plain that he wouldn't give away any clues whilst he pointed to a beat-up Chevrolet and told her to get in. A few minutes later, they lost sight of the town and turned onto a secondary road that led them across fields, all the way to the other end of the island.

"Are you sure you know where you're going?" she asked uneasily, seeing that he was walled in his silence as he drove along the tortuous path.

As suspected, she got no answer. Scared, she was ready to jump from the vehicle, but the sight of a large, illuminated house on top of a hill changed her mind.

As they neared, she realized that the windows were barred, and the facade was covered with bougainvillea. The mulatto honked insistently so as to alert the farmhouse's tenants, but no one appeared. Only some ferocious-looking barking dogs encircled the car. To her astonishment, Sonny went out to meet them and, murmuring a few words, which seemed more like passwords, managed to calm the animals down.

Anxious, Aline wondered what was going to happen next when she suddenly saw her husband cross the porch. She deduced from the relaxed manner of his walking that the latest deal had gone off without a hitch.

Marco opened the car door, as if nothing could catch him by surprise. He downplayed the fact that she was there and said affectionately, "You must be tired from the trip. Besides, the heat here is hellish."

Having said this, he opened a space between the dogs and made his way into the house, assuming his wife followed behind. Aline was not surprised by the welcome, for she knew that any reaction could be expected from him. She avoided engaging in useless reproaches and followed. She missed the previous nights' evening breeze at the farmhouse.

On crossing the threshold, she gazed at the exquisite decoration: Several watercolors signed by a well-known English painter based on the island hung from the walls; slender kentias stood out behind comfortable orange couches, and Turkish rugs in hues matching the paintings covered an immaculate marble floor. On top of these, low wooden tables caught one's eye for their arabesque drawings of great craftsmanship.

Curious, Aline peered up the stairwell's opening that led from the center of the hall to the upper floor and was amazed to see the assortment of oriental objects and statuettes that rested on shelves built into the thick walls. At the end of the spacious lounge, some sliding glass doors led onto the pool. Marco opened them. He suddenly took off his sarong and dived into the water naked to escape the heat and from having to face his wife. He realized it was impossible to avoid giving the explanations that he owed her, but the idea of having to do so and the danger that this meant for Aline terrified him.

With determination, he would eventually manage to get her out of his life. Only if he dumped her, or she managed to do so, would he save her from a more than uncertain fate. This unexpected visit meant an unforeseeable risk, but he realized that it would've been useless to try and prevent her from seeking him out.

Aline stood listening to the unmistakable thudding of the sea. They were on a cliff. Fighting back her resentment, she slipped out of her flimsy white dress and waded into the turquoise water to shake off the stifling heat. She then heard Marco's voice asking her ironically, "Are you more relieved now that you've found me?"

"I want to know the truth. That's why I've come."

The Foreigner, powerless in the face of unforeseen circumstances—for he never thought he'd love her so much—but certain that the following words would hasten her flight, began to make confessions not exempt from grief.

"I've been in this business for so many years…I don't even remember when I began. If you want me to tell you the truth, I don't know any other way of making money, and I conquered you with it."

And unable to hold back, he began to caress her passionately under the water. Aline, impervious, let him do and inwardly agreed with him. Her unexpected meeting Marco during those difficult days solved her financial problems and saved her beloved farmhouse from being sold.

Wanting to clear her ideas, she tilted her head back and submerged it in the water. On pulling it out and opening her eyes, she spotted a man stalking them from a corner of the garden. On being discovered, he approached the edge of the pool. Tall, blond, wearing cowboy boots and his gaze hiding under dark glasses, even though it was getting dark, greeted them with a simple shake of the head.

"Erik, this is Aline. She'll be spending the night here," Marco informed him.

"Okay," replied the stranger, phlegmatic. "Remember, Ahmed is waiting for us for dinner on his boat. Your friend is invited."

Having said this, he slipped away into the gloom among the dense vegetation.

Overwhelmed by the sinister personality of the newcomer, she wanted to find out his identity.

"His name is Erik Bürke, and he's the owner of this country house. In our circle, we call him The Norseman because of his well-built appearance and German nationality. He has a rotten temper," Marco answered. And without finishing the sentence, he got out of the water, tied the sarong around his waist, and took the shortcut to one of the guest bungalows.

She gathered her scattered clothes and took the yuccas-lined path, wondering what dubious ties bound the two men.

Marco turned on the ceiling fan and, to his wife's astonishment on seeing a kaftan and a necklace on the bed, he merely said, "Put both on. Erik has left them for you." And, without giving it importance, he continued, "He must've thought you didn't bring suitable clothes for dinner. On board the Ishtar, women tend to wear spectacular jewelry," and immediately noted, "It's a real diamond; don't lose it, it must be worth a fortune."

Aline figured it was no time to argue; she had other pressing priorities, but she couldn't help asking about his host, knowing she risked silence for an answer.

"That man would kill with a smile on his face; what business brings you two together?"

"His connections come in handy for certain operations, as mine are to him."

Those unusual statements put her on edge and made it clear that they were nearing the end of their story.

Suddenly, with the heat as an excuse, he turned off the artificial light, and the moon's reflections poured into the room.

"You aren't going to dump me now, are you?" He asked, for a moment regretting his previous provocations.

"Nothing will be the same knowing what I know," she refuted without daring to confess that she was not in love, although her husband was unaware of the sincere affection that she, despite his deceits, professed for him. Or at least that's what she thought.

"Are you ready?"

Aline didn't reply. At times he would ask without expecting an answer.

Downcast, they walked to the esplanade where Erik, sitting behind the wheel of a powerful SUV, was waiting for them. On seeing them, he started off raising a cloud of dust.

Marco, realizing that his wife dressed in the kaftan would have a hard time getting into the Jeep parked under the carob trees, took her in his arms and yearned for the days when this happened regularly.

The dusty road to the dock reminded Aline of the fear that gripped her on driving to the country house. This ride turned into a nightmare on hearing the Foreigner's words, which cut the silence short.

"Your life is yours, and no one can decide for you. With me, you'll never have a safe future. They might find us here tomorrow riddled with bullets." He paused and clenched his jaw angrily. "I'll never talk to you like this again. I think I'm having a moment of weakness and lucidity."

Taken aback, she realized that they had mutually lied to one another. He intentionally regarding his dealings, and she believing and making him believe that she was in love. Her survival instinct recommended that she dump him as soon as possible.

She got out of the Jeep, strained her eyes in a vain attempt to locate the Saudade, and was led to the most luxurious yacht on the dock, the Ishtar, escorted by the two men. Once on board, she noticed how Erik maintained a certain camaraderie with most of the guests. She could've sworn that he enjoyed introducing people much in the same way that her friend Doris showed her garden flowers in spring.

The Ishtar, like the Blue Moon, brought together the most eclectic characters that roamed the island. What did serious-minded, kif-smoking Arabs have in common with American painters or humdrum English businessmen with Oriental young ladies, she wondered? She was about to ask Marco when he, with some vulgar excuse, walked away. She figured that some big shot required his immediate presence.

Lost among strangers, she moved to the lonely prow. She leaned her slight body on the balustrade and watched the sea caress the rocks. Above, the ancient city was sheltered by long, illuminated walls.

A familiar sadness took hold of her, forcing her to think. Her inexperience threw her into Marco's arms, believing that he would protect her, but the only man who had ever done so was her father. The more she tried to get used to living without him, the more she needed him. She felt unable to calmly face the fond memories that often resurfaced. She wondered at what point he would stop being irreplaceable and, in an attempt to overcome her helplessness, turned her back on the shore. On doing so, she caught a glimpse of a man behind her who immediately introduced himself. Ahmed Rahhal, Lebanese, owner of the Ishtar, must have been watching her movements for a while. He exuded power, a power beyond the riches he obviously possessed. His authority floated in the air above good and evil.

His resolute, sensual gaze explored Aline's body, which could be discerned against the light through the kaftan's flimsy fabric.

"What can a woman like you pursue in the firmament that she doesn't find on Earth?"

She hesitated before answering him. She sensed that this man desired her, but what was he to understand about her life?

Unabashed, Ahmed continued to wait for an answer, and she had no intention of exposing her feelings to a stranger, but she quickly understood that, used to getting his way, he would not cease in his behavior. She acquiesced so as to put an end to the conversation.

"I'm looking for my father. Since his death, I try talking to him through the stars."

Rahhal turned pale, recalling that his own father had been killed one night in the desert. He was twelve years old at the time, and during his adolescence, when helplessness took hold of him, he would return to the mountains near Bhamdoum and spend whole nights seeking his advice in the immense star-studded sky. Why did that woman from a culture different from his bring to mind the most important event of his existence?"

It was painful for him to continue the conversation with the attractive stranger, and he bluntly lied to her about his thoughts.

"The stars don't speak," he answered to make the concept clear. "Besides…" he went on, seeing her sad expression, "it's important to be prepared for death, yours and that of your loved ones. We Arabs are taught that way," he stressed forcefully.

In a polite tone that admitted no reply, he invited her to accompany him up on deck, where he had arranged for dinner to be served. And aware that she was not among friends, she did as he bid.

Ahmed deliberately sat her next to Bürke, to whom he whispered a few words that were muffled by the music that filled the air along with the pleasant perfume of the red hibiscus that adorned the oval tables.

Aline hardly touched the exquisite food served by the crew. The oppressive heat did not subside. Marco's disclosures, compounded by her fatigue, had left her body battered. She needed to rest and return to the country house, but she'd never find "the house of the bougainvilleas" on her own.

Suddenly, the opportunity to do so presented itself on seeing her husband appear on deck with one drink too many. Taking advantage of this circumstance, she warned Erik of her leave-taking.

"The diamond you're wearing is of great purity, and it could be yours…" he whispered in her ear.

"In exchange for what?"

"In exchange for a night with Ahmed," he replied, unfazed, as if used to such exchanges and it were no big deal.

A chill ran down her spine. The feeling of being against a rock and a hard place seemed inconsequential compared to recent events and the proposal of the man in whose house she was going to spend the night. Around her, the guests were still engaged in trivial discussions, and Marco joined them. She was about to get up when Bürke grabbed her by the arm with strength and, in his unmistakable hoarse voice, spoke, "Take care of him. He's brash when he drinks too much. And do not forget my proposal. It may be of interest to you."

Any kind of answer would've worked against her. She remained silent.

She felt a rush of relief on leaving the yacht. Back on land, she wondered if it was all a mirage, but Erik's stocky figure on the deck, towering over the others, was real.

The Foreigner chose not to drive and showed her the way which, although the same, seemed more difficult because of the darkness. Far from imagining the Norseman's propositions, he deduced that Aline had overheard some conversation aboard the Ishtar when, point-blank, she asked him if his host provided women. He gathered the strength to continue with his plans and replied,

"He knows plenty of attractive young girls passing through the island, whom he introduces to his acquaintances, so he has influential personalities under his control. This makes him untouchable."

She kept silent, and he realized the danger that he himself was running when he had filled her in regarding his business dealings, but neither did he mind living without her by his side.

"And where is your boat?" she asked, on edge and surprised that the Saudade was not anchored on the island.

"It has set sail for Cinisi. Tomorrow, I fly to Milan, and you must return to our place in Rome," he answered, aware of the pain he caused her.

Aline, all of a sudden, fitted together the pieces of the puzzle stored in her mind even though—for reasons she couldn't quite figure out—she had always hoped to be mistaken regarding her suspicions.

She headed toward the bungalow. Throughout her married life, she had struggled to discover the truth, and now that he disclosed it, it came across as so brutal that she would've preferred to carry on ignoring it.

Exhausted, she fell onto the bed. She took off her necklace and asked her husband to return it to Bürke, silencing the latter's proposal. The idea of the two men clashing made her shiver.

She wanted to sleep, but the image of Ahmed on deck desiring her, in an attempt to buy her favors, only to receive a no for an answer, kept her awake. She closed her eyes. She wouldn't debate an agonizing situation and disappear just as she had come, and stick to her decision no matter what.

Marco turned on the fan and slipped into the bathroom. He had just played the last card to facilitate her freedom, but if Aline spoke, she wouldn't be safe anywhere. He stuck his head under the faucet's cold water. He was convinced of one thing: She would not betray him, and this would be her salvation.

On returning to the room, he was eager to make love to her. Watching her, he knew that he'd never love any woman as he loved his, and yet he was going to lose her.

Reality caused an irrepressible rage to take hold of him, and he stormed out of the room. With great strides, he made his way down the yucca-lined path to the drawing room. He opened the bar and poured himself an endless whiskey. The warm air turned oppressive. He stepped outside and leaned against the wall that served as protection against the cliff. He listened to the sound of the sea till Erik burst in, followed by his faithful dogs. With bloodshot eyes from the alcohol and with irrefutable firmness asked for something he never really wished for.

"Find me a special girl. I must forget Aline."

"Consider it done," he replied.

The Foreigner heard the footsteps of his host as he climbed the steps to the upper floor, where he had his private quarters. He suddenly felt the same way he did before he'd rescued her from the rowboat, cornered in his own loneliness.

CHAPTER 3

ROME, 1973

The taxi seemed to fly instead of rolling over the cobblestones of old Rome. It finally came to a stop in front of an orange building. Aline went in and climbed the stairs all the way to the attic. As she opened the door, she heard the phone ring and picked it up. Marco's nervous voice asking if she was alright made her assume that she faced more dangers than she had already imagined.

After a brief conversation—Marco hated long ones—she stepped out to the terrace and admired the domes and churches that seemed eager to hold time back. Those centuries-old stones contrasted with the interior of the apartment, bright and modern. He wouldn't be gone for more than a week, but this time it would be different. It would be the last time she'd wait for him. His trips were always a mystery, and his returns were unexpected. Despite his frequent escapades, Aline never got used to these inexplicable absences.

She would never rid herself of the anguish that Marco conveyed to her the day she urged him to give up his activities.

"I can't," he answered curtly. "This system is such that one can't simply get out when one feels like it."

After he'd uttered those words, fear took hold of her for good.

She stretched out on the terrace's swinging sofa and gazed at the twilight, as she used to do on summer nights at the farmhouse, and while reminiscing about the years spent with Marco, she took the categorical decision to separate.

She recalled her first months in Rome, a city that captivated her for its incomparable beauty and the open and relaxed nature of its people. With so much to learn and admire, she did not dwell on her husband's peculiar lifestyle. She attended language courses to perfect her Italian and spent hours visiting monuments and museums. She often longed for her childhood environment and would wander the city-center streets, where famous antique dealers displayed pieces that recalled those found in the farmhouse.

She'd never forget the unexpected vacations that Marco often organized to show her the country. Perhaps the happiest days of their marriage were those spent sailing off Capri. One of those nights, while they were dining in a secluded restaurant on the Neapolitan coast, he whispered in her ear how much he loved her. She would've liked to hold back the present because she hardly believed that anyone could love her as much as her father did. Arm in arm, they descended the steep alleys that led to the port, where the yacht awaited them. In the same cabin where he had brutally made love to her, he was now kissing her tenderly, sensing that their romance might come to an abrupt end.

When he insinuated this idea, Aline laughed and replied, "Don't worry, I won't run away."

But his grave face, telling her "you will," was etched in her memory.

It was a few months later, as they sailed across the Tyrrhenian Sea under stormy skies, eager to put in a nearby port as soon as possible when the opportunity arose for Aline to take a peek into the world of Marco's childhood. Although the Saudade anchored in a deep bay that guaranteed the needed protection, they chose instead to spend the night in a small hotel on the Sicilian coast.

A thick curtain of water fell on the fishing village where they found refuge, whilst the deafening thunder seemed intent on smashing the world to smithereens. Marco, reclining on the windowsill of a modest pension, called her to his side to share one of his deepest secrets.

"You see over there? My father was born on that stretch of land...he died young," he said, pointing to the island of Levanzo, which could be discerned on the horizon.

Suddenly the wind turned violent and forced them to take shelter, as if wishing to silence them.

"Tomorrow we'll set sail there. The people we'll be visiting will be happy to welcome us and to meet you," he added casually. But she knew it wasn't so.

Aline didn't think they'd be able to sail because of the storm, although, in the end, circumstances usually worked out in her husband's favor, and this time was no different.

The next day the scorching sun burned the stones, and the sea had lost its ferocity. They crossed its waters till they reached the island, accompanied by a cloud of seagulls flying in the same direction. He decided to dock far from the pier. He slung a leather duffel bag over his shoulder, picked up his binoculars, and, in a tone that admitted no reply, told the crew not to leave the Saudade. He jumped into a small boat from the steps of the yacht and held his hand out to help his wife. No sooner had she settled than they headed for the beach, cautiously navigating the waves.

Aline could've sworn that he gazed on the barren landscape fondly but kept her thoughts to herself.

They abandoned the zodiac on the sand and headed for the little village, which seemed uninhabited and quiet, but the echo of children's voices convinced her otherwise, and poorly dressed barefoot kids soon appeared. Marco asked one of them, who claimed to be the gang leader, to notify Don Giovanni of his arrival. Faced with the boy's obvious distrust, he gave him his name while he handed him a thousand lire, which the latter grabbed on the fly, disappearing into the village's twist and turns.

Aline took a look around, but nothing seemed to be alive in this clean, white, bright, and austere town. Who could live there? Intrigued, she was unable to hold back, and despite her husband's usual reluctance to answer her questions, she asked him about don Giovanni. He sat at the edge of a fountain in the town square, set the leather bag on the ground, and surprised her, just as he had the night before, by again sharing memories.

"My father was his right-hand man. He looked out for his interests. When he died, he took care of me as if I were a son. I'll always be indebted to him."

Aline avoided reaching the wrong conclusions, arranged her sunhat, and waited till an old convertible came around the corner. The young man who was driving it, seeing them, slammed on the brakes, jumped over the door, and came running toward them. He hugged Marco, and the two exchanged a few sentences in Sicilian. Introducing him to Aline, she noticed that he was a simple countryman, but his mettle and character were latent in every gesture.

Without preamble, all three got into the car and drove along the coast. They stopped in front of a house, the most imposing-looking and well-kept. They crossed a patio cluttered with flowers and entered the house, moving aside a quaint crocheted curtain. Dark antique furniture stood out in the living room. A woman dressed in black, fat and beautiful, despite her age, was waiting for them. She wrapped her arms around the Foreigner and kissed him affectionately on the cheeks. She immediately locked eyes with Aline and, changing her benevolent demeanor into a concerned gesture, hugged her. She assumed that Marco would want to eat his favorite fettuccine, and happy to satisfy him, headed for the kitchen to knead the dough.

The young man who had guided them to the house was joined by others who also enjoyed a brotherly friendship with her husband. After offering them some refreshments, they settled in the patio under a thatched roof that protected them from the relentless sun until Don Giovanni appeared, who, due to his corpulence, walked with difficulty and leaned on a cane.

The Don commanded Aline's great respect, even though she was hardly aware of the scope of his business and his status in the organization. His appearance was that of a respectable family man and seemed happy to meet her. His wife, on the contrary, was suspicious, for Aline was not Sicilian and therefore could not think or be like them.

They ate at a long, never-ending table set in the shaded part of the garden. The younger ones scanned the horizon, on the lookout for the slightest movement. Even the faint breeze seemed to be under their control.

When the men retired to the upper floor, Aline, clearly uneasy, joined the women to help with the dishwashing, feeling like a foreigner in the midst of people who spoke little and scrutinized too much. At nightfall, as they returned to the Saudade, she thought she was leaving an unreal world with no relationship to the present.

Back in Rome, the alarming events that gradually became part of her life convinced her that Don Giovanni was the head of the Santacroce, an important mafia family. Marco was part of it and, consciously omitting the truth, left her at a dead end.

While they were married, they frequented trendy nightclubs and spent evenings with actors and singers, friends of his. Marco Partana made good use of these contacts for his business affairs.

The night in Desiderio, a haunt located behind Via Veneto, marked the beginning of the end of their marriage. Aline stayed behind with a group of friends while her husband locked himself up in the club's private area, where he was in the habit of maintaining long conversations. She was taken aback when, in a break from the norm, he burst back into the hall earlier than usual and, losing his customary equanimity, grabbed her tightly and yelled in her ear, over the music's volume, to follow him. Aline did what she should've never done when given explicit orders by a man like her husband. She refused to follow him, still unaware of the dangers amid which they lived. Furious, he dragged her firmly and flung her into a car whose driver was waiting with the engine running. In a fit of nerves, she threatened to get out at the next light. Marco, beside himself, slapped her before the expressionless driver.

"Memorize this: You must do as I tell you." This was his way of protecting her, but Aline only grasped the full meaning a few hours later, on realizing the magnitude of what had happened.

A powerful tranquilizer that she took to help her fall asleep, mixed with the alcohol ingested, made her sleep well into the day.

It was two in the afternoon, and her husband was not at home, nor did she know when he would return. She left the apartment and wandered around the city for an indefinite amount of time, as she used to do as a child, when, without understanding the reason for certain things, she ended up taking refuge in the woods near the farmhouse.

On walking past a newspaper stand, she was struck by the papers' headlines. She was alarmed on glancing at them. She bought several copies, which she stuck under her arm, and headed to the park near the Villa Borghese. Sitting on a bench in the gardens, she read the various articles. In big headlines on the front cover, they all mentioned the murder of a mafia capo that had taken place the night before in Desiderio. They then went on to mention the well-known personalities who frequented the club. She was sure that someone was covering for them because, despite their presence at the scene, their names did not appear. Her mind processed her husband's unusual violence and the speed with which they ushered her into the vehicle that was waiting for them at the gate. She, who never drank, had done so the night before, and her defiance had burst forth, but she was unable to turn her eyes away from the evidence.

Marco was involved in this murky business, although no one would prove it.

As devastating as the events were, she was at a loss as to whom to turn to for advice, and in the event that she might do so, she'd be betraying him.

Dejected, she returned to the apartment and noticed the presence of some men who seemed to be keeping an eye on the entranceway. She hurried up the flight of steps and knew right away that he was home. She had quickly learned to detect his presence without physically seeing him. She found him in his room, impatiently packing his suitcase. Without being cowed, she flung the newspapers on the bed. All she got in the form of a response was the click of the briefcase's latches and a blunt mention regarding the people standing guard at the entrance.

"They will protect you till my return."

And she could no longer lie to herself regarding Partana's true life.

Shaken by the events, she was determined to accompany him on his next trip, but it did not occur to her that a few days later, on having carried out her objective, she'd end up in the farmhouse discovering that important drug cache in the Saudade.

She had fallen asleep on the terrace swing, and when she woke up, she saw his luggage at the apartment's entrance. Ibiza, her husband's confessions, and her night at the bougainvillea farm gave her the strength to get up. She needed a strong coffee before calling the secretary of Renzo Pisani, one of the most successful couturiers of the moment and Marco's acquaintance, to ask for an appointment. She had explained to her husband her intention to work because she knew that she'd need to be independent as soon as they separated. Initially, he had been reluctant, but ended up putting them in touch, thinking that if his wife kept busy, she'd stop meddling in his affairs. He was hoping that if she forgot about his business matters, she would come back to his side.

Having secured an appointment, Aline showed up at an old palace on Via Gregoriana, which had been converted into Renzo's luxurious atelier. The building consisted of three floors, and despite its restoration, it still preserved that splendid ancient architecture of the past. Embedded in the door, a golden dragon's head hid the doorbell. She pressed it and, while waiting in the vestibule to be received, took advantage to examine the daring and elegant dresses placed like works of art waiting to be purchased.

After a few moments, a door opened, and she was invited to the palace's rooftop, converted into a garden, where, stretched on a massage bed covered with a sophisticated fabric, Renzo enjoyed his daily massage. Aline observed the couturier's handsome face and fine wrinkles, each with its own story, she thought, all while he looked her up and down with interest.

"Marco has told me that you can do a good job, and I believe him." He breathed deeply to the rhythm of the pressure points of the young man who was manipulating his tanned body. "You have to learn quickly how to treat my clients, and you'll let me know what they like and don't like. The rest will be explained to you by Carla Vanni, the directress, but be careful, for she bares her teeth easily and doesn't bother to hide her nasty temper."

Renzo turned around, allowing for the Roman sun to brown his skin, and Aline realized that the conversation was over. She then slipped downstairs, wondering how she would go about working with such a peculiar character. That frivolous environment did not shock her because ever since living with the Foreigner, she had gotten used to dealing with all sorts of people. Deep down, what really worried her was how the Foreigner would react on learning that she was going to leave him, but whatever it took, she had to regain control of her life.

Lost in thought, she reached the old Roman stables, converted into the building's courtyard. She pushed the thick solid wooden door and, from the deathly silence that reigned inside the enclosure, stepped out onto the street's bustle; and once again felt the immense emptiness left by her father's death.

A couple of days later, she had her first meeting with Carla Vani. This time around, she waited patiently till she was escorted to the latter's upstairs office. Upon entering, she was faced with a woman in her mid-forties, standing with her hands on a table full of fabrics and sketches, talking with her collaborators. Aline was certain that it was the directness. She wore a sober dress, and extravagant costume jewelry hung gracefully from her stylized neck. Her hair tied back in a thick ponytail highlighted her harsh but beautiful features, and her body had the necessary curves that provided a natural harmony that her models lacked. She was the spitting image of glamor.

It was enough for Carla to take a look and exchange a word or two with Aline to realize that the young woman had a serene beauty, coupled with a strong personality. She knew the couturier's opinion; he had made it clear to her. Marco's wife would be of great use to them given her wide culture and innate elegance, essential requirements when dealing with their aristocratic and famous clientele, but she, of course, would not allow anyone to overshadow her. It was thanks to her hard work and dedication that she'd become the atelier's most valuable person, especially given her financial difficulties as a result of the detestable Second World War, when she had sought employment in the small workshop of the famous creator's mother in Naples. With great effort and an iron discipline, she'd gradually climbed the ranks all the way till the day Renzo could no longer function without her invaluable assistance, till shedding any vestige of those past hardships. Nowadays, her orders were strictly obeyed, and in between things, she briefly explained to Aline what her work would consist of.

A few days later, when she began carrying out her tasks, she was able to confirm how Renzo's warnings were being fulfilled. Carla saw in Aline a dangerous rival and found it impossible to restrain her jealousy. As a consequence, she frequently despised her work or told her off. Aline, cautious, chose to remain silent so as not to enter into controversies that would result in the loss of her position.

She figured that Marco would soon reappear, and facing their separation was an undeniable fact. That deep chagrin that took hold of her every evening on descending the endless steps of Piazza di Spagna made her long to have Doris by her side.

Doris Lambert was the friend her father was always able to rely upon. Their friendship dated back to their youth, when the Ashers lived in Paris. Samuel, Aline's grandfather, was a successful Jewish industrialist. At the beginning of the

Second World War, feeling harassed and learning that thanks to their Sephardic origins, he and his family could obtain Spanish passports, he handed his thriving business over to his partner without a second thought. The latter was more than glad to take advantage of the difficult circumstances that gripped Samuel and did not care to pay him a cent in exchange.

Samuel, a man with a strong personality, intelligent and adaptable, took drastic decisions that radically changed his future. In those crucial days, Doris' father, an audacious banker, played a decisive role in buying their Paris home and cleverly getting the money over to Spain. Their unwavering friendship survived the vicissitudes of war as well as the passage of time.

As a result of her father's will, Aline spent her entire adolescence with the Lamberts, considering them her only family. She would have been relieved to talk to Doris but was incapable of involving her in her current life. She also thought that it would've been difficult for her to understand how dangerous a situation she was in. She'd carry on eluding her questioning and lying to her outright. She had been doing so ever since she found out about Marco's dealings. She also hid the truth from her when the circumstances almost forced her to sell the farmhouse. She didn't want for the Lamberts to take on any more responsibilities than they already had and chose to deceive them.

It was in those turbulent days while walking the dogs around the farmhouse, while pondering how to get ahead without parting with it, when the Foreigner burst into her life, seducing her and solving her economic problems in the blink of an eye.

In the evening, when she got back from work in the atelier, she found Marco lying in bed, looking as if he hadn't shaved in a couple of days. She was not surprised, for she was used to his unexpected returns. She took off her shoes and warily collapsed by his side.

"Where have you been?" he asked, trying to kiss her even though Aline avoided him.

"I'm working for your friend Renzo."

"The fellow is rather weird and totally mad but has powerful connections in high society. If you're up for the challenge, there is nothing more to say. By the way, have you taken any further decisions?" He asked, uneasy, suspecting that she had and certain that while he was away, she had reconsidered her future.

He never asked twice; if he did, Aline quickly thought, it was because he required an answer.

Three years had gone by since the night she had, somewhat reluctantly, agreed to marry him. Now she was sure as to why she was going to leave him. She didn't beat around the bush and explained her reasons, knowing that he would understand, although she never thought that her husband would fall madly in love with her and was at a loss as to how he would react.

"What I feel for you, I'll never again feel for anyone," he answered matter-of-factly while he listened to her with unusual attention. On the contrary, he didn't hold a grudge.

He admired her body, the body that, ever since the day that he had picked her up on her rowboat, he'd yearned for like that of no other woman. He immediately realized that there was no more to be said regarding their marriage and abruptly changed the course of the conversation.

"Why didn't you tell me that Erik had offered you the dazzling diamond in exchange for sleeping with Ahmed Rahhal?"

He caught her off guard, but Marco was in the habit of jumping from one issue to the next without having concluded the previous one. It never crossed her mind that he would get wind of what had taken place on board the Ishtar. She ruled out lying to him because the question had been too straightforward.

"You know I didn't accept. Otherwise, we wouldn't be talking about it. I didn't want to tell you. I know you and know that you would've turned against Erik. I tried to avoid it. I don't like that man. I'm afraid of what he might do," she answered without hesitation and with aplomb.

"To tell you the truth, I can't believe he had the nerve to approach you with such a proposition, but when you left, Ahmed, who had no idea of who you were and even less what united us, confided in me his attempts to get you through Erik. I know him well. Rahhal would never attempt to possess the wife of a man with whom he has a friendship. And I, although it is superficial, have one. Besides, I noticed that he was more interested in you than in any other woman."

"Forget the past," Aline insisted.

Marco, in his own way, shook his head, and she noticed how the color of his eyes changed tone depending on the moment.

"Erik knew you were with me when Ahmed sought him out to be the go-between. He said nothing and played dirty behind my back. I know how to settle this unpleasant incident."

The Foreigner was used to danger and coming out on top of terrible situations; Aline, on the other hand, weighed the risks he exposed himself to, brazenly standing up to them.

She carried on, trying to persuade him, but he, ignoring her, declared, "He'll pay for what he did...Are you sure you want to leave me?" he insisted, in spite of having provoked her to such an extent to do so, that he himself could've hardly imagined.

It was inconceivable to live with him without admitting the illegality of his actions, and his wife would never do so. He, much to his regret, admitted defeat and the fact of losing her. Delaying it would've pained him even further. The phrase "I won't change my mind" that she had uttered, he was simply waiting for. Everything had been said.

He figured that they'd never make love again. Unhinged, he brought his body next to hers, lifted her dress, and in a split second, freed her of her panties. Holding her tight in his arms, he thrust his hips forward and penetrated her with violence, the same violence with which he clung to life. Aline, exhausted but aware of her husband's contradictory feelings, finally managed to free herself from him and, without a word, left the room to go sleep on the living room's pristine white sofa.

In the morning, Marco's sharp words seemed strange to her. He was not a man who liked defeat. Giving in was not in his nature.

"I've decided that you should live in our apartment till you've organized yourself," he said to her as he hurriedly packed his bag, thinking that for safety's sake, she should find another place. "I'll be traveling quite a bit and don't have time. Use our account till Renzo pays you a decent salary. My lawyer Sassari will take care of the paperwork. I shall agree, in principle, with whatever you propose."

He knew that nothing would persuade her to change her mind, and an amicable divorce was the least painful way out of his dilemma. As for Aline, she felt the situation gave her a respite. Still, with a thread of hope, she insisted that he erase the night aboard the Ishtar from his mind.

"I'll do what I think best," he replied grimly.

And immediately left the room, leaving Aline with the usual uncertainty. She, without realizing it, began to cry; she hadn't done so in a long time. The last time was ten long years ago, the day she had to leave the farmhouse after her father's death. She was walking away from the house with Doris and couldn't help but turn her head and see how she was losing sight of it…she thought she was dying at the time. The farmhouse would always remain in the valley, with its cypress-lined path, but Aline would never again walk that path with her father. The dogs, barking, did not move away from the car as it slowly descended the lane. Doris was driving stunned and helpless in the face of the tragedy but needed to reassure her friend, and whispered to her, "Jews are brave, and you must be so too, now and always."

Aline remembered that day and Doris' words. She reflected. Her father had raised her to be strong. A few months before he died, he asked her to recite Kaddish when his time came. Like on that day, she convinced herself that he, wherever he was, would show her the way. She was sure that this would not take long to occur.

CHAPTER 4

ROME, 1973

As if trying to knock herself out, Aline worked till exhaustion.

An important North American film was being shot in *Cinecittà,* and Renzo was the wardrobes' creator. The leading actress' constant whims drove him up the wall, and he was in the habit of having Aline present for the fittings. Thanks to her good nature, the latter was able to get the diva to let herself be convinced by the experts. Textures, buttons, and endless details were considered over and over again, fluctuating between the emotional instability of the American star and the creator's firm guidelines.

That day, she was the last to leave the palazzo. She had to wait till they were all in agreement. On her way home, exhausted, she realized that with all the hustle and bustle, she had forgotten to take the color samples that urgently needed to be delivered first thing in the morning at one of the workshops on the city's outskirts. Disgruntled, she retraced her steps. She did not like walking late at night on the empty streets.

Once inside the atelier, she crossed the halls and was startled on hearing murmurs coming from the floor above. She plucked up her courage and climbed the spiral stairs that led to a vast room lined with mirrors. She stopped dead in her tracks before the reflected images.

The naked bodies of Carla and Giselle—a well-known model—in an erotic play-game on the soft carpet unmasked Renzo's most effective collaborator's Achilles heel. A brief instance was enough for her to realize how the authority of Pisani's partner was vanishing; Giselle was in charge. Certain that their moans would muffle the sound of her footsteps, Aline did not account for Carla's sudden movement, which led to her discovery. The latter managed to hide her embarrassment, but not a cynical grin that betrayed her anger.

Aline looked around the baroque room, which seemed to have lost its harmony, given the disorder caused by the two lovers during their passionate trance.

"I came to fetch something," was all she managed to utter, flustered.

"No need to apologize," she replied whilst wrapping a cloth around her body.

She got up and lit a cigarette. Her inclinations could not transcend, neither to the atelier's staff and less so to Renzo. If he got wind of it, he would stop believing in her impartiality when selecting models. Losing control of the girls was not part of her plans.

Carla, used to overcoming setbacks, immediately seized upon an idea: An exchange of interests. Making the most of adverse situations was the result of years of wrestling with them.

"I will offer you something that interests you in exchange for your silence. I'll be honest with you. I can't deny a reality," she said, feigning a fictitious nonchalance. "I'll get you on the design team. It's what you like and have the talent. Moreover, we won't have to see each other's faces every day."

Aline, stunned, remained motionless. The proposition caught her by surprise.

"Do we have a deal?" And like a prowling panther, seeing that she got no answer, ordered her, "Make up your mind!"

"Don't worry, no one will find out," she reassured her after considering how the slip-up had turned out to be a fortuitous one.

She would not forgo the unique opportunity to work hand in hand with the couturier and couldn't care less about Carla's infatuations. Although the speed with which the latter settled the matter stunned her.

Aline left the women; a skinny Giselle unmoved lying on the soft carpet leafing through magazines, oblivious to their conversations—for she didn't understand a word of Italian—and the directress cursing in Neapolitan for having had one of her best-kept secrets revealed.

Back home, she thought about Marco. It'd been a while since she hadn't heard from him or his lawyer. She felt an urgent need to rest.

The agreement was not long in coming. Renzo called her and asked that she join his team, busy at work on the new collection.

Whilst working side by side with him, she discovered his human side. When he shed his haughty and mundane attitude, he was kind and close. He entertained people with irony-laced anecdotes that spread from palazzo to palazzo. The little setbacks were unbearable to him, and the big ones he didn't even bother to think about. She quickly learned to solve his problems, and when they accumulated, she'd turn to his partner, who, accustomed, ended up taking charge of the situation.

Pisani frequently traveled to distant places in search of ideas that, mixed with white powder and imagination, he'd turn into his future creations. Aline always knew about his trips; his addictions would catch her by surprise later on.

It occurred on a spring day, one of those days in which the city and its monuments are bathed in that unique kind of light that enthralls tourists. Carla rang her up at her apartment, where Aline drew late into the night. They hadn't seen each other alone since their encounter. The call appeared to be of a personal nature.

"Come by my office first thing in the morning. I have to talk to you." And without further ado, she hung up.

Aline, used to the atelier directress' quirks and mood swings, didn't make much of it.

The following day she went over to Via Gregoriana. She found Carla sitting at her transparent glass table covered with checks and bank statements. As a shareholder of the Pisani empire, she controlled every lira that came in and out with excessive zeal. At her feet lay Huber, her favorite Doberman.

"Sit down," she commanded in her habitual, imperious tone of voice that admitted no reply, "Renzo called me yesterday to tell me that he's moved into his Marrakech villa to design the new collection. I suppose you have noticed his unjustifiable absence in full creative development."

Aline nodded and refrained from making a comment, in spite of having noticed the couturier's strange attitude in recent weeks. He lived oblivious to reality. He, who was so methodical, demanding, and perfectionist, left loose ends that others, shocked, tried to string together.

Carla began to play with the lengthy necklace she wore, turning it over more than usual.

"I've checked with the pattern-makers the designs they've made based on his drawings, and they're not up to the marvels he usually conceives. I suspect something is amiss. I want you to go to Marrakech and find out what's going on." She paused, fanned herself with the bank statements, and sighed. "He has fallen in love with Guy, that French kid you've seen hanging around the atelier. I need his news," and, with a conciliatory gesture, carried on, "I live off this business and live very well. I will not permit this debacle, nor am I willing for him to screw up a collection for an ass he fancies, but I know that if he doesn't have it, I risk him not doing it. In that country, he evades all responsibility and finds the lovers he needs…they're cheaper there, or he takes his latest boyfriend, making it more exotic."

And as if she were used to talking about her partner's flings on a daily basis, she clarified with ease,

"In Europe, certain whims are costly," she said, stroking Huber's back with the tip of her heel, not for one minute doubting that Aline would comply with her orders.

Aline thought on her feet. She needed the salary, much higher than what was offered in her first interview, and besides, she shared an unavoidable responsibility in the creative process. The couturier trusted her.

"When must I travel?" she asked, worried about the possible consequences of Pisani's fling.

"Tomorrow," Carla answered. She got up, putting an end to the talk. "Keep an eye on him and call me. At this point, we can't afford to make a mistake or waste another minute."

The Doberman, imitating its owner, stood up and pushed Aline toward the stairs. Judging by the look of things, she concluded that Carla and Huber were way too similar.

MARRAKESH

Stepping off the plane, the thick air reminded her of the days spent in Ibiza. She crossed the city and, as on the island, experienced a sense of gloom.

Villa Malik stood out against a turquoise blue sky, and towering over the roofs, lofty palm trees rose as if eager to reach heaven. She went into the garden suffused with the smell of orange and lemon blossoms and crossed the silent courtyard graced with a fountain from which the gurgling sound of water was all that could be heard. She followed Ebrahim, the young Moroccan who had welcomed her and was now escorting her to her room. He disappeared in the blink of an eye, leaving her in a spacious room where the arched windows shimmered with the colors of the mosaics. Her bed was covered with rare silky bedspreads and mismatched cushions of different colors.

Aline undressed with the scent of flowers emanating from the courtyard. She proceeded to take a relaxing bath and, whilst immersed in the bathtub, wondered in what state she'd find the creator and how she'd go about handling him. After her bath, she chose some comfortable clothes and headed toward the hall, which bore the unmistakable imprint of the villa's owner. The furniture that he was in the habit of buying from Sotheby's mixed with the local antiques bestowed the exclusive mansion with an original flair.

Drawn by the beauty of the surroundings, she crossed the magnificent gardens teeming with dense vegetation till she reached the edge of a swimming pool surrounded by flat palm trees. There, basking in one of his favorite fads, was Renzo, tanning in the sun's dying rays. The evasiveness in which he'd fallen and his loss of contact with reality was such that he hardly wondered what Aline was doing in his Morocco home. It sufficed to exchange a few words with him to realize that he was on drugs. She figured Carla had hidden the thorniest issue. She noticed the creator's dilated pupils, unusual irritability, and lack of motivation. He wallowed in a fictitious bliss that was shared by Guy, who, by the way in which he behaved, seemed better equipped to handle the substances that they shared and accepted the state of his lover with passivity and a degree of indolence.

At dusk, Guy took off, leaving the two of them pouring over sketches, reclining under a candlelit tent and surrounded by the typical abandon that engulfed life in that country. Aline noticed that the drawings betrayed the ups and downs of the doses that he was in the habit of consuming. It was impossible to move forward, she thought, with that material. If the necessary measures were not taken, the fabulous business that depended on Pisani's inspiration would come crumbling down. Reconsidering the entire collection from the start was the only solution, and yet, there hardly was any time to do so.

Realizing there was little she could do there, she retired to her room. It was clear to her now why Carla was adamant that she travel to Villa Malik.

The next day, the young Moroccan appeared holding a tray with a hearty breakfast. Hermetic in his manner, he moved with the ease of a professional model. These traits were part of the essential requirements in the boys who performed tasks for the creator.

As Ebrahim was about to leave the room, Aline, half asleep, asked him to accompany her into town to run some errands. He nodded and left the room, nimbly moving his body under some exotic blue pants, a color that decorated what Renzo owned.

In the city, from a café near Jemaa Square, she rang Carla to update her on her partner's condition. Aline was given unequivocal directives. Without wasting a minute, she had to get a hold of the drawings and return them.

"And what do I tell him?" she asked uneasily, thinking of the consequences of leaving the lovers adrift.

"Given his state, use any excuse you think necessary," she answered with a cold voice, "that is if he finds out. And remember to tell Ebrahim not to let Guy out of his sight. Given the circumstances, it must be up to me to decide. Don't talk to anyone. I will take care of him and his excesses."

Huber's impertinent barking at the other end of the blower confirmed its owner's nervousness.

"Okay, I'll call you," Aline answered, wondering what Carla was plotting in order to solve the pressing questions ahead. But the enigma would not be cleared up until she landed in the Eternal City.

"Do so from the airport, no matter what the time." And, as usual, hung up.

Aline came out of the café and looked around for Ebrahim. Eager to put off what was dumped on her and seeing that the Arab had time—indeed, he seemed not to care—she suggested that he guide her through the souks.

Together they explored the crooked and somber streets, with shops clustered on either side. Discovering that city, its environment, and its culture gave her ideas that would later be of great use. At dusk, they retraced their steps till they were once more back at the square, where people milled around fakirs, snake charmers, and food stalls. Seduced by the environment, she let herself be carried by her discreet companion to the stall of his relatives. There they ended up sitting on two puffs, savoring a delicious Harira soup.

Aline, crestfallen by Renzo's condition and sure of having earned Ebrahim's trust, shared her suspicions and asked him about his. With his eyes veiled by melancholy, he made unexpected confessions that she sensed hid a request for help.

Deep down, he loathed Guy. Ever since he'd shown, the couturier's life had turned upside down. What used to be a good line of cocaine was now a planned suicide; his lover had introduced him to heroin. The latter, mixed with his usual dosages of various substances, would end up being fatal.

Aline sensed the danger in the same way that she had known when driving in the Jeep through the Ibizan countryside when she felt that her life and that of her husband were hanging in the balance. She tried to reassure her friend, assuring him that Carla would take charge of the thorny situation and that things would change. He has his doubts, and with an inshallah that came from the bottom of his heart, he assured her that it would be what God willed. He said so with conviction, turning his gaze toward the mosque reddened by the last rays of the sun.

The urgency to get back to Rome imposed itself. Wrapped by the radiance of the light, deep in thought, they made their way back to Villa Malik.

ROME

Aline felt nervous seeing the directress, with an irritated air, pour herself one whiskey after another with the same precision as she did her accounts. Getting ready for the approaching storm, she dropped into the armchair and, with an air of disappointment, handed her the drawings. Carla grabbed them with a restrained swipe and scattered them on the floor. As she examined them, her irritation grew.

"If we present this, we're done for!"

Huber began to howl. He did so when her owner lost her composure.

Aline conveyed her concern about Renzo and the drugs he was taking at the instigation of Guy, who had him totally under his control. Carla, absorbed, paced up and down amid the ill-fated sketches. She seemed to be more desperate about them than about her partner's fate. She suddenly came to a standstill and fixed her gaze at Aline, observing her in a peculiar manner. Huber stopped howling.

"The only possible option has just occurred to me. We don't have time to look for a designer, and we can't expect him to recover any time soon. You will take charge of the collection. You have imagination, you're persevering, and your ideas are valid. Besides, you've worked with him, you know the workshops and how they function…In a nutshell, nothing is new to you."

Aline tried to rebut what, by all accounts, was sheer madness, but Carla, ignoring her, carried on, "No one, absolutely no one, must find out that the ideas are yours. Draw, and when I give you the green light, deliver the material to the workshops. They won't suspect that it's not his instructions. They're used to seeing you come in and out with his orders. In a few days, you will return to Marrakech. Just play along, and what he gives you, if it's the same as what you've brought, throw it away. You get down to work, and I'll take care of my partner."

Slumped in the armchair, Aline posed herself the inevitable questions. How was she going to go about doing what was asked of her? He was unique, and so were his creations. Now he was failing because the wrong man was frolicking in his bed, but she was also aware that if the collection didn't move forward, it spelled ruin.

As if Carla guessed her thoughts, she confirmed, "The losses can be incalculable."

"And when he's lucid again and realizes the deception, what will we do?"

"We'll have finished and sold the collection by then. I will also think about how to make him see that he was in no state to create it."

She finished her sentence and offered her a whiskey, which Aline accepted to alleviate her anxiety. She agreed, for the very first time, with the dreaded directress. Time was not on her side.

On reaching her house, she collapsed on the sofa. She understood that Carla would turn to her. It was the perfect cover to hide the designer's condition. Accepting the plan, besides saving the atelier from a debacle, meant a challenge to prove her worth to herself.

Her father had always dared her. He would turn all efforts to achieve one's goals into an intense training in order to overcome life's trials and tribulations. As he had taught her, she would rise to the challenge.

She went up to the roof terrace. It seemed as if Rome slept at her feet, and the sky wished to cuddle her while the moon smiled at her. If nature protected her on Earth and her father from heaven, all would be well.

Before Renzo fell into that hazy state, prior to his collapse, he had given strict instructions to his assistants. The new collection would be African-inspired. Aline chose not to change the initial idea, thus not raising anyone's suspicions with odd changes, and would follow what he had arranged in his moments of sober inspiration. She consulted libraries, collected books, and locked herself up in her Via in Lucina apartment. She disregarded some fabrics and kept others. Her personal experiences in Marrakech facilitated the difficult task. Souks, landscapes, colors, and mosaics inspired her drawings. She had so much work that, for a while, she forgot all about the Foreigner.

Every morning she went to the workshops so that they began to make the sketches that she'd created during the night come true. During the endless meetings to determine whether she should shorten skirts or lengthen blouses, whether patterns should be printed higher or lower, Aline was plagued by doubts. What if the buyers, characters who, with a single glance, destroyed or extolled a collection, rejected her proposals? In the evening, when she left the palazzo, despite having absolute faith in what she was doing, she would have much rather had the couturier in her place.

The days rolled by quickly, and she had her doubts as to whether the unbeatable team would finish on time, but stitch after stitch, they did. The collection left for Milan-Paris with mathematical precision.

The last trip to Morocco was made to calm Carla's spirits, troubled by the foreboding that her partner would show up unexpectedly after Ebrahim's desperate phone calls. And on crossing the villa's threshold, she realized that the directress' premonitions were not all that off the mark. The creator had a well-thought-out script with no intention of changing it. She found out that very same night, over dinner by the pool, when he told her of his plan to return to Rome. She guessed why when she asked about Guy.

"He's taken a vacation," he announced, exasperated.

Aline figured that Pisani's exile was over. Ebrahim confirmed it when confiding to her about the lover's many quarrels.

There was no other way out than to notify Carla and confirm the latter's fears. At the other end of the line, she heard curses and the sound of chinaware shattering on the floor. She tried, in vain, to calm her down and realized the urgency of leaving the country before Renzo did. She thought it was absolutely necessary to keep him in the villa until the collection was sold and that he go to a detox center. She left everything in Ebrahim's hands and swore to him that normalcy would eventually prevail. Both were eager to convince one another that it would be so.

Drenched, she arrived at the atelier. To the skepticism for the approval of her work was added how to reveal to the famous creator, when the time came, that his sketches had been torn to pieces and that she had supplanted him. She took a look around. The few attendees authorized to witness the collection before the official show chatted under the Venetian lamp that hung from the ceiling. She ran up the steps to the first floor. When she had made sure that each model knew what to wear, in what order, and with what accessories, she went back down to the hall and sat on a step next to Carla.

Giselle was the first to appear, magnificent, wearing an impeccable safari jacket over wide pants. She was followed by Eva and Lynda, dazzling, in linen suits in different solar hues. Stella and Clio paraded in simple, flowy matching skirts with gold-trimmed sweaters that seemed luxurious when in fact, they were just everyday wear. Bermuda shorts in desert sand tones, blouses with trimmings, and T-shirts printed with figures of wild animals that gave a carefree touch that the clients liked so much. Carla stood tall like a sphinx, pad in hand, not missing a thing, until the end of the parade, when the evening gowns embroidered with kaleidoscopic stones, inspired by Arab mosaics, drew applause from those present. Then Aline was certain that the sketches conceived on the roof terrace would end up covering the bodies of the atelier's clients.

When the last model had gone by, the small group demanded Renzo's presence. The directress, unemotional, downplaying the matter, said, "Work has been hard, and the stress has forced him to take a break."

Nobody objected. Her commanding and convincing tone of voice reassured everyone.

As in every new success, they toasted with champagne while Carla and Aline waited to be alone to—hand in hand—plot the outcome of the tricky issue that obsessed them.

Once everyone had left, Carla double-locked the door to the room where the collection was kept, went up to her office and told Aline that she'd wait for her there. Huber stretched out in front of the closed door, intending to pounce on anyone who tried to trespass.

Braced for the harsh reality that was upon them, Aline climbed the spiral staircase, made her way down the mirrored hall, and walked into the pleasant room. At the end, on the wall upholstered with an expensive shantung, hung innumerable photos of well-known artists inscribed to the couturier, and in the windows of the palazzo, velvety curtains provided warmth and the refined touch that the two partners adored. Leaning against one of the bay windows, the directress could not conceal her anxiety, tying and untying knots with her usual pearl necklace.

"I have nothing to say. Well…you got it right. The collection is elegant, daring, and, of course, sellable. It could've been done by my partner since it's in his line."

Aline was relieved, but her calm lasted less than a sigh.

"Ebrahim called me to tell me that Renzo smashed the ancient Chinese vases yesterday…they're worth a fortune," she added.

This was nothing new for Aline, who knew his ups and downs, exacerbated no doubt by Guy's departure, but she began to wonder whether Carla had made any decision as regards the couturier's problems.

The directress would have preferred not to reveal her ties to Marco—it was what was agreed with him—but the matter's seriousness made him an essential pawn. She'd been trying for days to find out his whereabouts, but to no avail, and his wife would surely know where the hell he was. Having no other choice, she plunged into the unknown.

"Now, my dear, let's face our present dilemma. I have meditated, and the truth is that I could use Marco's help. But I have to turn to you because it's as if the ground had swallowed him up, and he's the only one who can get us out of this mess."

Stunned and unable to figure out what their relationship was, Aline wondered how he would fix the problem they were dealing with.

Carla's feline demeanor presaged the worst omens.

"You should be aware that Partana has always supplied him with the drugs. Given the circumstances, I know that he's the only one who can detain him in Marrakesh and give him what he needs till we've made our press presentation. This is no time for him to make any kind of public appearance. If it crosses Guy's mind to set foot in Villa Malik, your husband, with his persuasive skills and expeditious methods, will keep him at bay. He does favors, and I return them." Listening to herself, Carla couldn't help thinking of all the years she'd been laundering money for him through her businesses.

Aline had thought the world had opened up before her when in fact, she realized that her efforts to distance herself from the Foreigner had been futile. How could she have imagined that he supplied Renzo with the substances that were ruining his life?

Carla seemed relieved, having shared her rapport with Marco. Her impassiveness made Aline lose her temper and, feeling betrayed just as on other occasions and furious at being so gullible, confronted her. She pitied the couturier, who, despite his success, was now abandoned to the fate of his implacable partner.

"For your own good, I hope you find another alternative. You look for Partana. I have no clue as to where he could be," those were her last words before rushing out.

Exasperation did not prevent her from analyzing the unusual nature of her husband's disappearance. She cast aside conjectures of any kind, tired of her life being tied to his without even meaning to.

The directress' cat eyes shone and revealed something different, as if pressured by haste. Perplexed, for she did not expect Marco or Aline to abandon her to her fate, she sensed that she would not see Aline again in a long time. Her anger vanished the minute she recalled how Partana's wife had secured the collection that everyone in the atelier depended on. Moreover, she was sure that she wouldn't uncover her shady affairs. She'd keep quiet for Renzo's sake; she was fond of him and admired his work.

She called Huber and mixed herself a vodka and told herself that she'd come out of worst predicaments unscathed, and this would be no exception.

CHAPTER 5

SICILY, 1974

Partana drove to Palmi, south of Italy, and left his boat and crew in the port of Naples. He wanted no witnesses to his journey. Michele Sassari, counselor, and the family's lawyer, had summoned them to his office in Palermo. The trip was a perfect fit.

Erik's murder, scrupulously planned, had no reason to fail. His brother Luca—he called him thus, even though he wasn't—needed to be in the loop as to the strategy to follow. He hid nothing from him because they were like two peas in a pod.

His real father died in a clash between clans, and he had little recollection of him, although he knew that he was one of the few people the Don sought advice from and listened to. From an early age, Marco showed an unusual aptitude for mathematics and, at the express wish of his godfather, left Sicily and continued his studies at a prestigious Milanese university.

Upon graduation, he moved to Philadelphia under the supervision of an Italian-American family, relatives, and associates of the Don. He subsequently worked for that clan, which controlled gambling and narcotics in that state. He quickly assimilated the pillars on which his life would be based, gained an impeccable culture and a style of interpreting business in the purest Santacroce style. On his return, Don Giovanni confirmed with his own eyes that he had made a wise investment. His godson stood out with his presence as a top-notch executive, and his contacts in the USA would come in handy. He had a knack for negotiating with people in key positions, which would greatly benefit the family's influence and power.

Every time he landed in Sicily, it reaffirmed Marco's desire to end his days on that island where he felt deeply protected. Although he roamed the world and lived far from the peaceful countryside, the mob's mindset always went with him like a second skin. The codes of honor, fixing the bloody slights unofficially, and the certainty that in the face of any offense, the family would do justice on its own terms gave him confidence. He didn't believe in anything else.

Thus, Erik's days were numbered; his life was in Marco's hands.

He had no difficulty, first thing in the morning, finding the address that Luca had given him on the outskirts of Palmi. When he arrived, he came across two armed men at a door with tall wrought iron bars who asked that he identify himself. They moved aside and escorted him to the extensive plain within the property. He figured that the area covered about ten hectares of land, protected by a high fence. In the distance, amid the sprawling nature, he beheld the ancient and imposing residence. The helicopter and pilot were waiting for him to fly to Cinisi. They would land on the spacious rooftop of Luca's villa, built by the sea, thus leaving no indication of his visit to the island.

For the entire length of the ride, in accordance with the organization's credo, the pilot remained silent. A silence that allowed Marco to meditate. Beneath his feet lay the turquoise sea, and in his mind, Aline. The conviction that the decision that they'd both taken was the only viable one was a truce, of sorts, in his life, which of late had turned into a meaningless coming and going, plagued with inconceivable risks. Perhaps if he were killed, it would put an end to the hell his existence had become since his breakup with Aline.

He made love to women who were captivated by his appeal and his money, but none of them had been able to make him forget his own ever since the day he rescued her from that other sea, now distant for him. He hadn't had the slightest doubt, from the moment he took her hand to help her aboard the Saudade, that she was his destiny. And no one ran away from him. Of that, he was convinced.

The helicopter settled with a gentle sway on a spacious roof terrace converted into a helipad. Marco alighted and walked quickly to the house's lower floors. Of a linear structure and well sheltered, it bore no resemblance to the Don's Greek-style mansion, which stood in the countryside near Bologneta. His brother required security and speed to escape, as he moved large amounts of drugs from Sicily to America and Europe.

That morning, settled in the kitchen, they caught up on the latest operations while they savored the *granita* that Marco missed so much. At a certain point, once the usual matters had been dispatched, Marco laid out the reasons for which he wanted to take revenge upon the Norseman. His brother smiled, thinking that he'd do the same. The latter immediately enquired if the Don was au courant, as it was risky to go about it on one's own, but Partana convinced him that, given how he was going to proceed, he wouldn't find out. Of course, if he were to state his intentions, he might be refused, and this did not fit into his plans. He also knew how much Luca enjoyed risk; he courted it.

"You see, I enticed Bürke into an operation. I've provided him with invaluable contacts over the years, and he trusts me," he stated. "He must deliver sixty kilos of cocaine to some Dutchmen who, in a few days, will be in the port of San Antonio aboard the sailboat Gull. They've given him a significant advance. If he doesn't deliver, they will eliminate him. I will not deliver the goods to him, and, of course, no one knows that I'm behind this."

"Why don't we take care of it? My men wouldn't fail," Luca pointed out thoughtfully. After all, disloyal Erik was not governed by the rules of the mafia.

"It's not possible. The arms trafficking network, of which he is a powerful link, would investigate. If we do it as I tell you, no one will ask any questions. In a few days, he will start to get nervous. He will go to my apartment." His face twitched. "I must return to Rome and get Aline to safety."

"By the way, why don't you take her to Zumikon? I've got a house there. It's perfect for disappearing. It is not far from Zurich. It's a gated community, I'd say idyllic," he hinted without showing the slightest worry.

The Foreigner considered how best to convince her to come with him. Aline had figured out the hornet's nest they were in the day she accidentally discovered the stash in the Saudade, but now it was different, for she made her decisions without consulting him. Still, if he conveyed to her that they were both in danger and misled her as to the real reason for the trip, she might not object to accompanying him. In a few days, it would all be over. He always got his way, and this was a matter of honor.

He went toward the terrace and looked through the bay windows to watch the surroundings. Luca, noticing that he was unusually restless, assured him of the presence of several armed men placed at strategic points. They did not lower their guard. Seeing that they were late for their appointment, he got up.

"Come on, finish your coffee and let's get going to Palermo. Sassari is waiting for us, and then we will have lunch at a friend's restaurant near the Borgovecchio market." He put his arm around his shoulder affectionately and led him to the front porch.

Before getting into the Mercedes, Marco made sure that the pilot was to be on the terrace at the appointed time to return to Palmi. Followed by the bodyguard's vehicle, they took the highway to Palermo.

The office of the lawyer Michele Sassari was located in an old building in Via della Libertà. He himself opened the door. In his stony gaze, one could discern the type of man bestowed with the resolve to make certain decisions without batting an eye. Marco considered him an intelligent and persuasive man. He was not impulsive and was able to judge his adversaries. He trusted him blindly and had, on more than one occasion, shown his staunch loyalty toward the family, taking untold risks to defend them. To catch him off guard was a real achievement.

Over time, Marco reached the conclusion that if Michele needed to resort to a law and it didn't exist, he'd invent it.

The room, crammed with books stacked on shelves up to the ceiling, impressed the Foreigner. All three sat around an oval table cluttered with papers. The lawyer gathered several stacks of folders to make room for the glasses and fresh lemonade he had had his secretary bring. He did not beat around the bush and delved right into the matter at hand. He wanted to sound them out, for Don Giovanni was meditating, pulling out of the drug trade, and busing himself with less risky activities more in keeping with his current life-style. Money was no longer an issue; there was plenty.

Luca did the numbers and gave his opinion, at first forcefully and then with the same violence as the island's volcanoes. He went against his father's sentiment, for he felt the business was well established, and it had taken years and too many lives to accomplish this. Marco replied that the situation had to be assessed calmly and, for a split second, imagined that this new scenario might allow him to get Aline back. The same amount of time it took him to rule out such a possibility.

The conversation lasted long enough to ascertain the earnings they'd lose and the risks they'd no longer have to take. When Michele deemed the meeting over, Marco sensed that the consiglieri and his godfather had already given some thought to the idea. Nothing was conceived in haste in the organization. He drank a sip of the delicious lemonade while Sassari updated them on the latest business structures that allowed them to launder, through real estate, the large amounts of money obtained. The support of high-level politicians that the Foreigner provided was essential.

As they said goodbye, the lawyer hugged them in a brotherly manner, as was their custom. Escorted, they stepped out onto the bustling street and walked leisurely to the Borgovecchio market, where they mixed with the crowd, stopping at the fish and local produce stalls. They reached a small restaurant, where they were escorted to one of the more secluded tables. The pasta with sardines that Marco hadn't tried in months tasted heavenly, and the Sicilian wine mixed with his brother's intimacies took him back to his youth on the island.

"You know..." Luca confided in him, "the owner here had the brilliant idea of sticking the drugs in sweets. He set up a company that exported them to America in beautiful gift boxes. I guess you could say that he's a man with bright ideas."

Between anecdotes, ricotta cake, and grappa, Marco tried to loosen up while he listened to Luca, who was intent on convincing him of the importance of not dismantling the excellent structure in place that sustained their business.

Marco let him open up. At the end of the day, the Don would work it all out.

Evening fell. The bodyguards informed them that their contacts within the police had alerted them about the checkpoints that had been set up on the motorway leading to Cinisi and that they'd have to take a different route on their return. It was agreed that it'd be best to go through the interior of the island, although this entailed a delay that worried Marco. Aline was in no imminent danger, but it was only a matter of time before Bürke went haywire.

They left Palermo behind and took the narrow road that wound up the mountain. A fine rain began to fall, and gray clouds covered the sky. Luca was driving the Mercedes, and he hit the accelerator. He liked taking that route at breakneck speed, which the powerful engine allowed for, and Marco's urgency to return to Cinisi was the perfect excuse. He was as fond of Bellocampo's curves as he was of those of women. He used to say: "If you grab 'em well, you'll reach a safe harbor; if not, you can fall into the abyss."

Although Marco was befuddled with his plans, he warned Luca that he was driving too fast; however, his brother replied that he was capable of driving that route blindfolded. To satisfy him, he took his foot off the accelerator as he entered a sharp curve, and while he continued to close the turn, occupying part of the oncoming lane, a truck suddenly appeared. Luca tried to avoid the collision but was unable to do so. The car plunged headlong down the precipice below, flipping several times, to end crashing into the trees.

It began to pour. The bodyguards, who were in another vehicle, first confirmed that the truck driver had died and then descended the precipice until they reached Marco and Luca. Hardened in experience, they realized that the two were badly injured and unconscious. One of them stayed behind while the other went off to get help.

In no time, the Don was informed of the seriousness of the accident on the stormiest night in recent months in Sicily.

ROME

Aline headed toward the apartment. She was just as despondent after Carla's revelations as she was the night Marco abandoned her in her beloved farmhouse after she'd stumbled upon his stash. The same impasse, with the only difference of having gone through traumatic experiences. She had just come face to face with the last link of the inevitable.

She rescued from her memory the peaceful evenings at the farmhouse and the simple phrases with which her father instructed her. He taught her to choose freely and to assume her responsibilities. This time around, she'd failed, but wouldn't let her despondency confuse her. Straightening out her life far from Partana was fundamental. She figured that her mistakes were part of a learning process that one must necessarily go through.

She needed a refuge and to think. The farmhouse awaited her.

She hastily climbed the old-fashioned steps of the apartment with the idea of leaving as soon as possible. The door was ajar. Uneasy, she gave it a light push without moving from the landing. A pair of cowboy boots that were familiar to her protruded from the sofa and looking up, her fears were fulfilled. Sitting there was Erik Bürke, tanned from so much sailing and surlier and harsher than during the night she dealt with him in Ibiza. With a gesture that admitted no reply, he invited her to close the door. She obeyed. There was no way out. Tense, he stood up and took a few steps toward the two majestic Buddhas that graced the corners of the entrance of the dining room. He seemed more corpulent than what she recalled of him the night aboard the Ishtar.

"I've come so you can tell me where Marco is. He has to deliver some merchandise to me." In fact, he thought that finding her had been an advantage because if she was there, that meant she was still together with Pastrana. Before forcing the door, bereft of reason, he hadn't the slightest idea as to who he'd run into.

Aline, who clearly understood that one put one's life on the line when making deliveries, began to feel that hers was in danger if she didn't tell him what he wanted to hear. The Norseman, no doubt, was at wit's end. Specifying what he expected from Marco was clear proof. She was seized with fear. If she tried to run away, Bürke would grab her in one move. Plucking up all the courage she could muster, she repeated what she'd said to Carla in the atelier, "I haven't the slightest idea as to where he could be. Why don't you ask his people?"

"They're not clued in. This is something between him and me." That phrase aggravated the scenario. "Come closer."

She thought it best not to contradict him. Deep down, she asked for God's help. She had never turned to Him after her father's unfair death, but no one else at this point could work a miracle.

She repeated the truth. She did not know where the Foreigner was. She felt a sharp blow to the head. Lying semiconscious on the floor, she opened her eyes and saw Erik's face grazing hers.

"Tomorrow, I'll be back early, and if you don't tell me, I'll kill you."

Numb and unable to utter a word, she heard the footsteps of his damn boots and a threatening phrase in the distance.

"Don't try to escape. I'd find you faster than you can imagine."

She heard the sound of the door closing. A terrifying malaise settled in her body. She had a hard time getting up and, dazed, made her way to the bedroom. She parted the curtains and saw a car stationed on the street with two men inside it. That was enough for her to realize that it'd be impossible to leave through the main entrance. In the bathroom mirror, she checked to see that she had no sign of violence, only her face transfixed by panic.

She knew that her husband wanted to take revenge on the Norseman the minute he learned of the proposition that the latter had made to her, treating her as if she were a prostitute. But knowing the rules of the game, she was sure that either her husband or his right-hand men would have alerted her and gotten her out of the apartment before choosing not to deliver the goods. Marco always kept his end of the bargain and never left her unprotected. Those gaps which didn't quite fit made her fear the worst.

She concluded that her plans were unfeasible. Impossible to get to the farmhouse, now turned into a deadly trap, or to take refuge in Paris and expose the Lamberts. She didn't know who to turn to. A phrase the Foreigner had uttered in the air while she was driving the Jeep in Ibiza echoed in her memory: "They might find us here tomorrow riddled with bullets."

It was fear that made her remember the letter that Doris had given her years earlier and that she consciously left on the desk of the little stone house. Her father asked her in those lines that in the face of any kind of adversity that she should turn to Patricia; "Her experience and milieu will be crucial," he'd written. She decided to follow his advice, convincing herself that the last person she should turn to, much to her regret, was the lover she never cared to meet. Not even after his death, when Doris had tried, given the great friendship that existed between them. Life itself led her where her father had wished.

She tried to keep cool. To get in touch with her, she needed to call the Lamberts. She loved them too much, and Bürke would clearly carry out his threat. On picking up the phone, she realized that the wires had been cut. It was getting dark. She turned on several lights so that the men standing guard in the street wouldn't suspect while planning her escape. She changed clothes: Jeans, low-top loafers, and a thick sweater, and grabbed a purse, her credit cards, and a flashlight. She then went to the kitchen. At the upper end of one of the walls, she saw the small window that her husband had barred, but behind one of the bars, there was a lock that was hard to see if one didn't know of its existence.

"You never know which way you'll have to escape," Marco used to say.

From that spot, she'd be able to get out of the mousetrap that, in no time, the apartment had become. She opened the window, slipped through the gap, and after carefully closing it, fell onto the neighbors' roof.

Sore from the fall's blow, she crawled forward, afraid that if she stood up, Erik's men would see her silhouetted overhead. A few rooftops away lived a drunken, bohemian painter. The house was familiar to her because, sometime earlier, in the hope that they'd buy a painting of his, he'd invited them to his studio, and Marco, every time he came across artists down on their luck, he'd buy several canvases no questions asked.

The attic consisted of two rooms separated by a corridor, and Aline noted right there and then that the windows were identical to those in her kitchen, except that the painter's had no bars; open in summer and closed in winter. She had to reach them. She kept stumbling along, gathering dust and scratches, till she breathed a sigh of relief on seeing that the little trap doors were wide open. She figured she was lucky. It was spring. She switched on the flashlight and made a quick scan of the room. She nimbly slipped through the opening and carefully landed on the ground so that no one would hear her. She wouldn't have known how to justify her inexplicable entry into the house, but the fear was so great that her anxieties were trivial.

On slightly opening the door, she caught sight of the artist's mane falling behind the chair. He was peacefully sleeping off his drunkenness. In front of him, the television broadcasted a soccer game. Aline tiptoed over, dodging wine bottles, paintings, easels, and brushes. She realized that her clothes were all dirty after her rooftop trek. She tripped over a motorcycle helmet and, without a second thought, picked it up and put it on. This way, it would be harder to recognize her.

With her heart in her mouth, she left the door ajar in case she had to retrace her footsteps and hide in the attic. It all depended on how far the car with Bürke's men was stationed and how watchful they were of the entrance through which she was planning to escape. She stopped at the doorway, saw some tenants coming along, and took advantage of the opportunity to go out into the street along with them.

She did not look back. At a brisk pace, she reached Via del Corso, dumped the helmet into a container, caught the first taxi she came across, and told him to take her to Termini Station. She'd go unnoticed amid the crowd. She welcomed Rome's chaotic traffic and the daredevil driver behind the wheel.

Before stepping out of the car, she made sure that no one had followed her. She ran into the terminal and, luckily, came across a phone booth. Relieved, she dialed the Lamberts' number. At that hour, Doris was in the habit of preparing dinner in her elegant Paris house, which had once belonged to her grandfather. The phone rang three times, and she then heard her friend's voice at the other end of the earpiece. Without preamble, she asked her to warn Patricia of her imminent visit, all while keeping an eye on the passersby.

"You'll have to go to Como. Ask for Villa Balbini. It borders the lake; everyone knows it, and Patricia too."

Doris immediately realized that something was amiss from the trip's haste and from the way in which she spoke. She asked why she was going where she never wanted to go in the past, and Aline omitted the truth, just as she'd been doing ever since she discovered the Foreigner's fraudulent life.

There were no more trains for Milan, so instead, she rented a car and headed north on the highway. The long hours that awaited her driving alone to her destination were conducive to stringing her thoughts together so as to forget about Bürke and reminisce about her childhood.

CHAPTER 6

UPPER AMPURDÁN, 1964

The cypress-lined path linked the old farmhouse to the little stone-built house. Her father used it as an office during his stays in the Ampurdán, and there the two held their endless talks.

The little house with its thick oak door consisted of two floors. A ground floor furnished with leather sofas, an English desk, and his favorite paintings, and a staircase that led up to the upper floor, a loft where he had assembled his private library. The roof was hidden beneath the branches of an enormous fig tree, which in summertime she'd climb to hide amid its branches and listen through the open windows—given the suffocating heat—to the long conversations her grandfather and father carried on. They never discovered her, which allowed her to compare her world with that of her ancestors, who, despite being close, she felt he was distant.

When their reunions came to an end, her father would go back to his work or simply carry-on reading, while she'd take the path that led to the farmhouse and try, in vain, to attract her mother's attention, who was spending less and less time with them. Aline, much to her regret, became used to the maternal absences and eventually looked forward to them, for they allowed more time with her father.

After the forced flight from France, Samuel, the grandfather, did not waste time or stir up the past. He directed all his energies into his family's well-being and starting anew. In the back of his head, he kept the formula for the industrial treatment of steel that had made him rich in France, and nothing prevented him from putting it to good use in the new country. Once settled in Barcelona, he rented some warehouses not far from the port and began to temper steel metal with salts applied to thermal oils, thus increasing its hardness and strength. The risk-takers who, once the war was over, resumed their business activities were greatly impressed, and his company went on to prosper and grow throughout the country.

Katinka, the grandmother of Russian origin, was dodged by a deep sadness the very day she set foot in Spain. As an Ashkenazi Jew, she did not accept her husband's impositions, who forced them to quit practicing their faith. Henry made an effort to obey the patriarch without questioning his judgment because he knew that the circumstances had forced him to make such a difficult decision; however, he treasured the teachings that his mother bequeathed him in a corner of his heart. Thus, his behavior would always be based on the values that she, with so much love, had instilled in him, values that he would later transmit to his daughter. No one perceived his intentions except Samuel, who, over time, resigned himself to accepting that Henry would not change his mind.

Henry Asher, Aline's father, had a brilliant career as a lawyer and, in his field, was considered one of the best. At the death of the patriarch, he sold the company and wagered the profits acquired on wise investments that increased his assets. Distinguished looking, he possessed a self-confidence that people immediately noticed. Moreover, the different assimilated cultures conferred him a unique charm.

Katinka had already died when Henry married Isabel Caralt, a stunning beauty who came from a ruined aristocratic Catalan family. They were not Jews; had the old lady known, it would've made her misery all the greater. Betsy, diminutive by which she was known in her circles, saw in her future husband the intelligent and fighting man who, even though young, enjoyed an excellent economic position. She realized it wouldn't be easy to stumble upon another man like him. To win him over, she projected a personality that had nothing to do with her real self; she assumed a role that she figured was best suited to her ends. She had an innate gift of being liked by those around her. But, stripped of her roles, she was cold and manipulative, traits that were accompanied by a good share of psychic instability that people mistook for a will to live. Few really got to know her, and even fewer intuited her true personality.

He realized the ruse when his daughter was born because it was from then on that Betsy felt safe and began to show her real self. Faced with this new reality, Henry reached a series of compromises that, if it hadn't been for the girl, he would've never accepted. He ignored her lovers and the way in which she went about squandering money, and she, in return, was happy to relinquish the role of mother in exchange for money and freedom.

As soon as she had the use of reason, Aline sensed that her parents must have ironed out their differences in private, for they never argued, and it was obvious that daily events had been resolved beforehand. They attended unavoidable social gatherings and fulfilled their obligations, but each one went about their life without interfering with the other. As a child, Aline adapted to the unusual situation, and when she was seized by sadness, she'd take refuge at the top of the dense tree that protected the stone house with its branches.

When she'd come into the little house, Henry made sure to instill in her his beliefs and principles, and she'd listen with great attention and respect. "If you don't know where you come from, you don't know where you're going," he'd tell her. He carefully related the family's history, his life in Paris, and why they left France. He also confessed that he believed in God and was sure that He'd protect her.

All this gave her self-confidence but also taught her that one must learn to lose and start anew, just like the patriarch had done. Her father raised her responsibly. One day, on the boat of José, the fisherman, he said the following:

"If you decide to be Jewish, it won't be easy, and you'll have to be brave. You won't be able to shirk your duties neither with yourself nor with others; think about it." But when he saw the effect that his words had had on his daughter's face, on reaching the shore, he jumped into the shallow water and, lifting her up, hugged her tightly.

The faint glow of the stars lit the beach.

The farmhouse that she adored was decorated without haste. She admired her mother's exquisite taste when combining objects that she acquired on her trips with original regional pieces, making the Ampurdán property one of the most coveted. English chintz upholstered the sofas, and the old-fashion restored fireplace was framed by shelves chockablock with books from diverse points of origin. Paintings by Meifrén and Constance on top of the Catalan chests of drawers and furniture purchased from the antique dealers in Kensington Square formed a harmonious and warm ensemble. Katinka's old rocking chair stood by the fireplace. Her son would sit on it at night and read by the fire the way his mother used to do on bleak winter nights. When the north wind burst in, Aline, sitting on the rug next to the dogs, listened to the stories that her father told her about her grandmother, whom she had never met.

Once settled in Italy and married to Marco, she was tempted to make changes to the decoration but refrained because everything reminded her of her happiest years. With great effort, she repressed the urge to take away what her mother left behind, for she didn't want to erase the days she lived with her father.

The patriarch would've preferred that Aline grow up absorbing his directives, but she only seemed to understand her father and the freedom he gave her. Between grandfather and granddaughter, a river without bridges was created, and each one walked along different banks. That didn't stop Samuel, with his presence, from replacing the gaps of affection that Betsy left in her wake.

Together they planted fruit and vegetables in the orchard near the old farmhouse, and he'd tell her of the hours Katinka spent picking beans sitting on her stool while the chickens scampered around her. At dusk, they fed the fish in the pond or hunted frogs hidden under the water lilies that croaked too loud, keeping them awake at night. Despite carrying them in buckets to the nearest river, the green amphibians inevitably returned to settle in the small lake, something that neither of them understood.

Unlike the boisterous excursions she went on with her father, the walks with her grandfather were marked by their quiet composure. Aline had always admired him for his confidence and the courage with which he'd overcome his misfortune.

Of that dramatic period, only Henry had the privilege of speaking to him about it. Aline's father was a lawyer who did not want to let go of his faith, and Samuel, a successful entrepreneur more inclined to abandon it since the very moment he was forced to flee Paris. For years they avoided discussing the subject, despite their discrepancies, till the day when they no longer could avoid the confrontation, as Samuel kept seeing his son instilling in his granddaughter those beliefs that he, Samuel, thought better left behind. Those conversations that she listened to attentively, hidden at the top of the fig tree, fascinated her and led her to understand the different cultures to which she belonged: That from which she came, the one she was living, and the third and most difficult, the one her father proposed to her: Meditate, assimilate and, finally, choose.

She remembered the hot summer night when her grandfather entered the little house with an air of gravity, leaving the door ajar. She pictured him settling down on the worn-out leather sofa and, despite the crickets' chirping, she could hear their conversation in French, the language they chose for their dialectical battles, and which she spoke with the same fluency as Spanish. As opposed to what had been the norm, this time around, her father lost all patience and, with a forceful phrase, put an end to the discussion.

"Aline will be educated with complete freedom to choose. No one will impose anything on her. You yourself have lived through experiences that forced you to make choices that went against your will." He added a pause in which Samuel's usual replies couldn't be heard, and it even seemed to her as if the crickets had fallen silent. He then went on, "I'd swear that deep down, in the bottom of your heart, you don't disapprove."

The patriarch, who felt old and tired, rose and, without refuting him, returned to the farmhouse along the cypress-lined path. It was one of the last visions Aline had of him.

The gentle summer peace was interrupted by the arrival of the Lamberts: Doris, Pierre, and Valerie, their daughter, who became Aline's comrade. Both took advantage of the freedom they enjoyed in the old farmhouse. Nobody questioned their escapades. Those comings and goings, where the two pulled the nets with the fishermen and had breakfast in the port tavern to end up bathing in the peaceful coves, made Valerie feel like an adventurer, and she'd look forward all year-round to her vacations in the Ampurdán. They used to go on long bike rides with Pierre, leaving Doris and Aline's father exchanging confidences that lasted entire afternoons. Their long friendship was consolidated over the years. Her father avoided returning to his old home in Paris, and when he traveled to the City of Light, he met Doris anywhere except at the house on Av. des Sycomores. The dramatic days lived between those walls weighed like a slab on his memory.

A year before her father's untimely death, Aline noticed that he was doing more traveling than usual and had lost that melancholy air that characterized him. The reason caught her unawares in her hiding place. Doris and her father talked happily inside the little house. She could've never imagined that he was madly in love with a friend of the Lamberts. Her name was Patricia, although everyone called her Pat. She lived in Como, and she deduced that she must've been the reverse of her mother's medal. The discovery provoked in her such a deep hatred for the stranger that, in order not to have any more disappointments, she gave up climbing to the top of the fig tree. She withdrew into herself until a few months later, in an outburst, confessed to knowing about his relationship with Pat without confessing as to how she'd found out. He didn't ask and tried to explain that nothing was going to change; she pretended to understand. She didn't mention Patricia's name again, and neither did she return to her hiding place. Had she done so, she would've learned the way in which he went about protecting her and making sure there were no loose ends in regards to her future.

Just like the Libeccio wind, which one can see coming, Doris sensed at the beginning of summer that he had something serious to tell them when Henry summoned her and Pierre to the little stone house. Her friend knew how to deal with difficult matters, explain them and leave them legally closed. The obstacles which he'd overcome, in addition to his efficiency, endowed him with special skills for solving complex problems. This was a case in point. Over his favorite appetizer, he filled them in on his will and explained why he stuck to its unconventional clauses. If he died and Aline didn't bow to her mother's demands, the latter would try by any means to destroy her. She used to do so with those who didn't comply with her wishes. She'd make use of her sophisticated and deadly charm, her beauty, and her cunning to destroy her. It would be hard to get out of the bottomless pit into which her own mother could throw her.

"I am going to leave my estate, which is important, to my wife. Except for the farmhouse and some securities that will go to my daughter; in exchange, Betsy must agree that you get custody of her until she comes of age. If she refuses, she will only get the legal portion. I'm sure she'll choose the money." His eyes had a sad undertone. "I am aware of what I'm asking of you, but my wish is that she has you by her side."

Doris, who was French but British in her upbringing and reserved in her emotions, could not contain herself that afternoon and threw herself into her friend's arms. Then Pierre, getting over his bewilderment and wanting to calm both of them, spoke in a conciliatory tone. "I know your wife," he said, omitting the fact that she had tried by all means to get into bed with him, "and I think you're doing the right thing." He emphasized that if anything were to happen, Aline would be one more member of the family.

The sentence that followed left the Lamberts speechless.

"I have serious heart problems," Henry confided with feigned calm.

It seemed as if time had stopped without daring to continue. Henry Asher did, "If anything were to happen to me, I want you, Doris, to reveal Betsy's true identity to my daughter, so she can protect herself. Aline suffers from her indifference but is unaware of her wickedness. At present, I act as a barrier, and my wife sticks to our agreements without meddling in her life. Swear to me that you will."

"I shall do so. And Pat?" she hinted.

"She knows nothing. I want to live the time that I've got left without either of them knowing what could happen."

All three exchanged knowing glances, but after the arduous conversation, their idyllic summer was truncated. The scale of the secret altered their mood, despite doing their best to hide it.

They sailed across that sea, which seemed to hide the secrets of the world, swam in deserted coves, and ate on José's large boat. Their afternoon games of *pétanque* were well-known in the village, and in the evening after dinner, they listened to Mozart while playing chess, but a sense of unease hovered above them.

Betsy, oblivious as always to the vicissitudes that took place between the walls of the farmhouse, did not pass up any social event, alternating them with her trips. She hardly flinched on learning about the stable relationship that her husband had with Patricia. On the contrary, it was convenient for her. She was backed by the conviction that he would not abandon his daughter.

Aline, who was unaware of the truth, continued to come and go between Barcelona and the old farmhouse and, while trying to figure out her mother's attitude toward her, kept hating her father's lover and missing her grandfather, who had never made life difficult for her. She did not share any of her secrets with Valerie, for she was convinced that her friend wouldn't possibly understand what lay behind her family's veneer respectability. On the other hand, over the years, a strong complicity developed with Doris, who, moreover, fulfilling her promise, revealed the reasoning that her father had entrusted her with.

The hours that followed her father's death left Aline in a state of utter exhaustion. After a few days, the excruciating pain gave way to the first memory of him. It happened on the morning that she left the old farmhouse. The dogs howled behind the car as it slowly made its way down the cypress-lined slope. She didn't even have the strength to answer Doris when the latter assured her that the Jews were strong and that she had to prove it, but deep down, she gave herself an ultimatum: She was not going to wallow in gloom. He wouldn't have liked to see her in that pitiful state.

The ride from the Ampurdán to the Barcelona airport seemed eternal, just like the flight to Paris. The sense of helplessness was ever present, and she struggled in order for it to not gobble her down.

PARIS

Doris got out of the car on Av. des Sycomores and clutching Aline's hand tightly, she said, "I want you to feel at home. After all, this is where your grandparents and father lived. You've returned to your roots, and that's the important thing."

The white, stately house with the slate roof appeared before her as beautiful and welcoming as the scant descriptions that her father had given her. She stood for a long time before the building, contrasting reality with his stories, till Doris' voice brought her out of her reverie.

"Come on, we must start the day-to-day," she told her with absolute determination, hugging her.

Slowly, and with the Lamberts' support, she faced her father's brutal absence and her mother's unjust behavior. The latter chose the money. Ridding herself of her daughter was a relief since, in her plans, she intended to spend long periods in Venezuela, where her latest conquest resided.

Aline recalled the impact she felt on entering the house. The sober, elegant, comfortable home was surrounded by a garden with abundant flowers. An oval drawing room decorated with empire furniture left behind by the Ashers, mixed with other pieces acquired later, took up the left wing and communicated with a spacious dining room. On the opposite side was the ample kitchen. Opposite the noble front door, on coming out of the drawing-room, wide, carpeted mahogany stairs led to the upper floor, where the bedrooms were located, and at the top end was the attic converted into a pleasant room. She was quick to reply when asked where she preferred to sleep. She chose the attic.

The Lamberts enrolled her in Valerie's same school, and overnight her friend's orderly, methodical life became her own. At night, before falling asleep, she spied the starry sky through the glass of the attic window. She had admired those stars with her father when they went fishing, walked the dogs, or swam on the beach late at night. She trusted that the messages transmitted to the tiny stars would reach him, and she never fell asleep without first sending him one.

After several months of lethargy and confoundedness, she began to question Doris about the house and her grandparents. She took advantage when the latter knitted near the bay windows, lying on the sofa, while the cats played with the skeins of wool. She didn't deny her any answers and ended up loving her deeply.

One cold winter afternoon, as the snow slowly covered the garden, Doris showed her the corner of the living room where her grandfather and father played their games of chess while Katinka cooked Ashkenazi-style chicken and mushroom soup. She mentioned how many times she ate that soup and the evenings shared with her grandmother.

"What are your memories of Katinka?"

"Blonde, with wonderful blue eyes. Energetic and sensible. She didn't talk for the sake of talking, and when she did, she carried a heavy Russian accent. She cherished solitude and suffered the anguish of being Jewish. The opposite in her personality to that of your grandfather, who, as a good Sephardic, talked non-stop, and his emotions were skin-deep. From the moment they realized the urgency of having to leave France, they both changed. Katinka never shed her sadness, and Samuel worked around the clock in his new host country."

The memory-laced afternoons unfolded, and Doris told her everything, from her parents' agreements to Betsy's emotional instability, which was not exempt from evil. Aline, who had already suffered her mother's scorn and abandonment, acknowledged that her father could not have left her in better hands. She didn't mention her again.

Living in the same house that her family was forced to flee from made her reflect. In their flight, her grandparents could've never fathomed that their granddaughter would one day reside in the same place in which they were both so happy and so wretched. And as Aline and Doris pieced together experiences of that period, she felt she was Jewish and wouldn't cease to be.

It was as if the heavens had parted when she first met Haim Weiss, a few years her junior, the son of some friends of the Lamberts. His father was the cultural attaché at the Israeli Embassy in Paris. Haim became her confidant, and they began a deep friendship. He had pale skin, light eyes, and red hair that immediately struck her. His face was covered in freckles. He was a physics student and excelled, thanks to his outstanding grades. The overflowing energy that he radiated helped her overcome the most difficult period in her life.

It was he who, along with other men, was in charge of reciting Kaddish for Aline's father at their synagogue on the Rue de la Tournelle. The day Aline asked him why they frequented this one and not any other, he answered categorically,

"It's where the Ashkenazi go, which we are, and so was your grandmother."

So, Aline imagined Katinka offering prayers in the solemn synagogue.

The afternoons spent sauntering in the *Bois de Boulogne* seemed too short, given all the wisdom he imparted. This bond was further strengthened by her thirst for knowledge and his willingness to help.

Shortly after explaining why he was living in Paris with the Lamberts, Haim, who discerned a Jewish precept in every circumstance, appeased her.

"Don't worry; when a Jew dies, the soul protects those who stay behind." He then clarified, "But whenever you are in physical danger, ask God to help you. He hardly ever fails."

From then on, she was certain that her father's spirit would protect her wherever she went.

Her visits to the synagogue and to the Weiss family home became more frequent. She noticed that her new friends' convictions were identical to those her father instilled in her, and she was to meet people who had overcome the same sort of hardship that her grandfather had gone through. Her first Sabbath took place at their home. Doris did not intrude or inquire about her visits to Rue Gustav Doré, where her friends lived, near the embassy on Rue Wagran. They were respectable people who would no doubt help her friend's daughter, guiding her through her beliefs.

Several years, more or less pleasant, elapsed. Aline finished her design studies, learned English, and took Hebrew language classes. Valerie begged her to accompany her on her outings, but Aline chose to stay chatting with Doris or take long walks accompanied by Wind, the puppy that, born in the farmhouse, she'd taken to Paris.

Henry's death, the different cultures in which she was raised, and the family conflicts she'd gone through turned her into an adult before her time.

One afternoon, while baking a cake, Doris asked if she wanted to meet Pat, but Aline refused; she had always viewed her as a threat to her father's love.

"Someday, you'll have to," Doris whispered.

Aline thought that day would never come.

When Pierre, who worked as a biochemical researcher at some important laboratories, was able to free himself from his job, they'd escaped to French Brittany. The landscape was nothing like the coves and forests of the Costa Brava that she missed so much, but neither she nor Doris were in a position to live within the walls of the farmhouse or walk along the cypress-line path; much less could they have borne entering the little stone house. She would return a year before her encounter with the Foreigner.

PARIS, 1970

Aline left the Blvd. de Montmorency behind. Sitting in the taxi on the way to the airport, she reached into her jacket pocket and took out the amulet that Ali had given her an hour earlier. She experienced a strange feeling on looking at it. She unfasted it and saw that it carried some Arabic language inscription that naturally she did not understand.

She remained looking at it for a few seconds, but her concern for her beloved farmhouse ruled out her attention from anything else.

A few days earlier, upon returning to the Lamberts, she came across a letter on the chest of drawers in the hall. The return address belonged to a Spanish law firm. She hesitated before picking it up, but couldn't resist her impulses, as if a bad feeling took over her will. The letter was addressed to Pierre, who, since Henry's death, managed her estate through the Barcelona law firm. The pages read in haste in the attic conveyed that the securities on the stock market had suffered significant losses. They advised selling the farmhouse to obtain liquidity and thus cover their expenses. Her recent coming of age entitled Aline to give the appropriate orders to her managers. She would order them to no longer send her accounts to the Lamberts. She no longer wished that they assumed any more responsibilities on her behalf. She would hide the disaster, but under no circumstances would she part with the farmhouse. How she'd go about doing this, she'd figure out at a later date. Doris' absence during those days made things easier for her. She had little trouble convincing Pierre of how much she longed to be back at the farmhouse, and he, knowing what it meant to her, encouraged her to go. Aline, aware that the lawyers would soon be calling, arranged for her departure in a flash.

She reminisced about her last hours in Paris as the taxi drove to Orly. She'd left her suitcase in the stairwell and, given that there was no one in the house, decided to go for a snack at the brasserie on Rue Poussin. During the short stretch till the bistro's threshold, she turned in her head hypothetical solutions that would allow her to keep the farmhouse but found none. She settled down at a small table and ate a croquet-monsieur, constantly mulling over the problem. When leaving, she waited to cross as there were no traffic lights. She cast a distracted glance at the opposite sidewalk, which was oval-shaped and wide, abutted the intersection between the two streets.

Just at that point, she spotted some Arab women surrounded by children. She knew them by sight since they lived nearby. The house in which they lived, magnificent in its dimensions and finishes, housed countless relatives who spent long periods in the capital. She never had the slightest idea as to what rank the skinny boy with floppy ears whom she came across on a daily basis had in the endless family structure. The same one she now saw playing around while the women gesticulated in vehement conversation.

No one took any notice of the large van parked, blocking the view of the cars descending from the Rue Poussin. It all took place in a matter of seconds. The Porsche was coming at great speed, and something caught the boy's attention across the street. He bolted without looking at either side. Aline pieced together the fractions of seconds in which she had a presentiment of what was going to happen if she didn't act quickly. In a flash, she ran toward him and caught him in midair as the car brushed past them and continued on its reckless course. She felt the pain in her side from the blow as she hit the asphalt and the screeching of the Porsche's tires echoed in her ears.

She recalled the shocked faces of the women as they picked up the unharmed boy, the thanks that came from the bottom of their hearts, and the difficulty she had trying to convince them that she was capable of returning home without help.

"You risked your life to save Ali," one of them mumbled, flustered, helping her. "He's my son."

"No one saw the danger. There was no other choice."

Leaning on the extended arms offered, she made an effort to get up; she yielded to their pleas and gave them her name and address since they wanted to thank her family for her risky gesture.

Ali took advantage of the commotion that had formed on the roadside. He slipped away and approached her, handing her a square bronze tag that hung from a leather cord. With curly hair and sparkling eyes, he spoke in fluent French.

"It's my amulet. Wear it always. It will bring you luck."

Aline took it in her hand but told him not to part with something so personal; but, without waiting for an answer, the boy returned to his people. She, bruised and under shock, continued toward Av. des Sycomores. If the car had taken that turn, but a few seconds earlier, she wouldn't be where she was.

The pain from the impact was increasing, as did the bruises on her left leg, which grew larger and darker by the moment. She shrugged it off, but as time went on and her leg grew numb and swollen, she began to fear the worst. Would she endure no matter what till she reached her destination? The important thing was to arrive.

The plane took off smoothly. The solid impression that a long time would pass before she returned to the house that had belonged to her grandparents overwhelmed her. As well as the why. She was far from foretelling that during her stay at the farmhouse, her rowboat would go adrift, and Marco would appear and change the course of her future forever.

She looked out the plane's window, and all she saw were white clouds.

CHAPTER 7

COMO, 1974

Aline arrived at Villa Balbini at dawn, through mists, a safe place, provided Bürke had lost her trail. In any case, the fog had been her great ally.

Meeting her father's mistress under such circumstances made her uneasy, but he left proof of that desire in his last letter. His reasons, as was always the case, would be justified, and she would soon discover them.

Dawn was breaking. She plucked her courage and got out of the car. High walls finished in natural stone pillars with a wrought iron gate opened onto a small atrium, largely occupied by a round pond. The lawn adorned two side aisles sheltered by cypresses, placed in a straight line all the way to the main entrance. Aline was puzzled as she moved forward. Her farmhouse was rustic, cozy, and wild. Villa Balbini, regal, exquisite, and aristocratic; they were different and yet had the tall cypresses and pond covered with water lilies in common.

The symmetrical facade stood out for its beautiful ocher tones, and the main entrance was framed by square stones of the same grayish color as the window moldings. A mountain range jutted out behind the villa, and Aline assumed it went all the way down to the lake. She hesitated before ringing the doorbell, but fear drove her to do so.

On the fourth ring, she heard someone approaching. A woman opened the door with the unmistakable air of being the housekeeper. Slender with graying hair, she scrutinized her with languid eyes, as if wanting to buy time while deliberating what best to do with her. On seeing that her interlocutor was still silent, Aline, with irrefutable kindness, spoke, "Could you please warn the lady? Tell her I'm Aline Asher," and waited for her reaction.

The latter, on hearing her last name, immediately made a gesture that could be interpreted as "come in."

Aline entered a wide hall, the heart of the property. On each side, one room led to another, and at the end, a large window framed with brightly colored curtains looked out onto the garden and lake. All around her, the walls displayed *trompe-l'oeil* frescoes in warm tones of honey and orange. She couldn't help looking up to admire the wonderful Venetian chandelier hanging from a spectacular ceiling decorated with paintings of clouds and angels. A central table on a Persian rug and some bergère chairs decorated the hall. She was alone, and the temptation to open the doors to admire the surroundings overcame her. The grass, like a tapestry, covered the ground up to the iron verandah. A few meters away was the lake, and in the distance, the mountains that ended up submerged in the opaque waters. The landscape radiated stillness.

A part of her father's existence that she had always denied and that now intrigued her was beginning to manifest itself. Chance led her to where he wanted and where she sensed that he'd been most happy. Memories of her childhood filled her head that she hadn't been able to shake off the previous night, forcing her to reckon with her past. She always censured Pat, unable to admit that it was she herself who did not want to share her father with anyone. Whereas the unknown lover knew how she lived her role and let them live theirs. As she contemplated the waters, which were neither turbulent like those of the Costa Brava when the north wind blew, nor clear like those of Ibiza, she thought about the importance of verifying if indeed he'd made a wise choice.

She heard her name being called. She turned on her heels. Blonde, charming, and stylish, Patricia Di Borgo was approaching from the garden. Her heart skipped a beat when she stood before her. Her smile disarmed her, and with a sincere gesture, she hugged her and told her how happy she was to have her at home. Aline, who was used to remaining calm, was at a loss and without arguments to justify her sudden presence.

"I know these are ungodly hours, but there was no choice," she answered, feeling guilty for having come looking for her only out of necessity.

Pat didn't ask for explanations. She fixed her sapphire eyes on hers, took her by the arm, and suggested that she rest for a few hours, without telling her that right on the veranda where they were, she'd promised Henry that she would become friends with her when the time came.

They entered the villa from the park and reached a patio that was used as an informal dining room whenever the weather permitted lunch under a wisteria-covered pergola, whose clusters fell faintly on a granite-top table. They walked through the deserted kitchen and up a wide staircase to a landing that led to her bedroom. Pat pushed open the door and, with a quick glance, made sure everything was in order whilst deducing that something sudden or dramatic must have occurred for Henry's daughter to show up at her house at dawn in such an unsettled manner. As a woman of the world, she concluded that the next few hours would be decisive in order to get to the bottom of this affair.

Aline went up to the window. The light of day slowly dispersed the fog and multiplied the warm yellow tones of the curtains and bed covers. A vase of flowers on top of the French chest of drawers and a chaise longue made the room look cozy. She put her bag down and heard Patricia say in a subdued voice, "rest," while she quietly left the room. Aline was grateful. She immediately forgot about Erik, about the drugs he was looking for, the Foreigner, Carla and her futile attempts to locate the latter; of her aborted trip to the farmhouse, of her attempt to change her life and subsequent struggle to save it after the clash with the Norseman. She fell into a deep sleep.

SICILY

Sassari, the lawyer, was driving in a hurry to reach his destination. The truth is that it was becoming an uphill battle having to follow Don Giovanni's orders.

He'd never met Aline and knew nothing about her either, since her husband had always kept her far from the family. The reason why had always remained a mystery, but the Don respected his godson's wishes, provided they did not hinder their shady business affairs. The terrible events befallen boiled in his head. Marco's sudden death, torn asunder by the impact, and Luca's pain when he woke up from the never-ending operation had altered his mood to the point of needing medication to sleep.

Don Giovanni, secluded in his mansion in the middle of the Bologneta countryside, was tormented by the death of whom he considered a son. It caught him by surprise, as if he'd received a bullet shot. And it was quite a while before he came to terms with the fact that Luca, due to his complex injuries, would take months to recover and that Partana would no longer be in the meetings or act as a go-between with the upper echelons of the business and political world, essential for their affairs. He was irreplaceable. He now rested on his beloved island. Michele was relieved that it was so.

The family vault received the coffin at the express wish of Don Giovanni, followed by a solemn funeral. Everyone attended, but only Aline remained oblivious to the events despite the fact that he tried to locate her in vain in her Roman home. And if during the night of the accident the storm swept everything in its path, the day of the funeral dawned calm.

Marco and Luca had grown up together, and there was always a special affinity between them. Over time, the former made the contacts and organized the transactions; whilst the latter executed them with his men. When Marco was orphaned, he was taken in by the family. Michele figured that the Don had seen innate qualities in his godson, which, as was later proven, served as a springboard for the Santacroces to expand their operations far from Sicily.

After the first few hours of lethargy caused by the painkillers, Luca asked about his brother. In the end, Michele had to break the news to him himself, in the same way that in the face of difficulties, legal or not, he had to be present. The Don's son, dejected and worried, harbored serious difficulties in speaking, but the urgency with which he required the lawyer not to move from his side put the latter on guard. He sensed that perhaps Marco had left some loose end that the family was unaware of. No sooner had he left the hospital room than he realized that Partana, even though he was dead, would keep them all on their toes.

After listening to Luca's explanations and the Foreigner's failed plan, which had left his wife in a vulnerable situation and them too, he had no choice but to declare to the Don's son that future instructions should be given by his father, not without before admonishing him firmly for taking unnecessary risks. The latter, aware of the disaster, accepted reluctantly. The matter which seemed simple enough with his brother alive now seemed extremely complicated.

Michele was forced to report to the Santacroce's pleasant country villa after leaving the hospital in the evening so as to bring Don Giovanni up to date on the situation. The latter, crestfallen by the recent tragedy, received him in the large office where they'd plan their strategies, discuss conflicts, and enjoy successes. Don Giovanni, despite his age, kept his cunning and intelligence intact, and as a Sicilian, understood right away why Marco would want revenge but was outraged that he had acted behind his back. Nobody had ever dared do so. He picked up a Havana cigar, lit it, and pondered the facts without uttering a word. The problem required swift action for several reasons.

The first was that if the merchandise was not delivered, Aline's integrity was at risk, and he was aware of the importance she had in the life of his godson.

Second, Bürke was moved by self-interest since he was acting on his own, behind the organization's back; the danger was that different rules applied.

And lastly, he would not allow for a plan in which the chances of failure had not been considered to breach their security. The circle that Marco had left open when managing his personal and economic interests had to be closed. In due time the Norseman would disappear without a trace in the sea's deepest end.

Sassari accepted his boss' invitation and dinned with him while they listened to their favorite opera. This meant he didn't wish to talk but rather to reflect. When it was time for coffee, the two men returned to the office. In a deep voice and with a hatched plan in his mind, the Don gave him detailed orders, not without first giving his own assessment of the situation, as was his wont.

"Michele, it's not a complicated matter, but it could be if mistakes are made. I trust you. Marco wanted to avenge his honor. I will respect his wishes and act. The difference is that I've thought things through before making decisions. I don't think he did."

Troubled, he confirmed the obvious. A difficult and fluctuating time for the family was upon them until they found if at all possible, someone like Partana.

Michele went over each order received. Salvatore, Luca's best man, would handle the job alongside him. Every minute was calculated. Nevertheless, he realized that the slightest unforeseen event could derail the execution. The accident was a perfect example.

When he left the mansion on his way back to Palermo, he cursed the Bellocampo curves. He urgently needed to contact Salvatore and question Luca to find out where the merchandise was that the Foreigner planned to deliver to Bürke for the latter's downfall. He slammed on the accelerator and began his countdown.

Salvatore was well-built, of medium height and dark skin, with bushy eyebrows and a flattened nose from all the blows he'd received. He was in his element when it came to drugs and the underworld. He could kill better than anyone. When given the order, along with three of his men, in the dead of night and with lightning speed, they tore down a wall to recover the drugs hidden inside Prizzi's rural house. The merchandise was then hidden under some vegetable boxes in a van that was transporting groceries to the port of Marsala. It ended up on a fishing trawler, along with two other fellows, all presumably on a fishing expedition.

In the moon's absence, the night was serene and dark. They cast their nets into the sea and waited a while until a fourteen-meter sailboat appeared, advancing with solemn slowness, fluttering a French flag. A zodiac was lowered and, with two men in it, headed at half throttle to the trawler. Salvatore stalked like a hungry wolf, attentive to the slightest movement, although he'd been informed that no one would be patrolling the coast that night.

Paul, the Marseillais skipper with an introverted air and plenty of experience in this type of commission, came on board. Together they oversaw the exchange of merchandise and counted the hermetically sealed bags that contained the entire stash.

The Santacroces had overpaid for the cargo and informed the Marseillais that it was traveling without an exact delivery date. They weren't actually going to go through with the transaction until Aline showed up. Nevertheless, Paul considered that the risk of waiting was worth the amount contracted. And so that there be no setbacks and knowing that Salvatore was a man of action rather than precision, he thought it appropriate to point out, "It will take me three days to anchor in Es Vedrá. Try not to be delayed."

"I hope I won't," he replied, thinking that locating Bürke would take an imprecise amount of time.

Faced with the unforeseeable, they all went their way. Salvatore returned to land. A car drove him to Luca's house, whose slow recovery prevented him from leaving the hospital. He had been a step away from death, and it was slowly dawning on him. His people gave Salvatore a hearty dinner and a comfortable room. As one of Don's trusted lieutenants, he followed orders without asking questions. Neither did he like to think too much, but he suspected that the unexpected operation could be related to some unforeseen event caused by Marco's sudden death. The family moved amounts much higher than that stash through different and safer channels. What would have prompted them to do such an operation? He didn't trust the Norseman; if it were up to him, he no longer would be alive, but he'd been forbidden to kill him.

He got into bed and didn't wake up until dawn when he heard the sound of the helicopter landing on the rooftop. He had a strong coffee, and, despite the high wind that threatened the stability of the flight, he refused to delay it. He traveled the same route Marco had a few days earlier but in the opposite direction, landing on the same esplanade. Two men were waiting for him. They patted each other on the shoulder and climbed into a powerful Mercedes under a bleak, cloudy sky. Salvatore sat in the back seat drowsily and only came around before the Foreigner's apartment in Rome, whose keys jingled in his pocket. Michele had given them to him when he suggested that he meet Erik in the attic. He felt his stubble, got out of the car, and ordered his people to find the Norseman and bring him back as quickly as possible. He couldn't be too far.

He opened the thick, dark-green front door and stepped into the hall, feigning indifference. He climbed the high steps all the way to the top floor, introduced the key into the lock, and opened it. Everything seemed in order. The apartment was not large, and thanks to his experience, it was easy for him to verify that there was nothing that compromised the organization. He immediately lightened up. The Don's godson memorized facts, dates, and names better than anyone else; he had no need for agendas or scraps of paper. Each agreement was closed verbally. This intangible way of proceeding avoided future inconveniences. On discovering the cut telephone wires, he let out a *managgia la miseria* and wondered if that had anything to do with Aline's absence. He had just found out about that marriage from Sassari a mere few hours earlier. Everything continued to appear very strange to him.

He killed time under a relaxing shower. Next, he simply decided to wait on the spacious white sofa, the same one where Erik lost his temper when looking for Partana. Waiting was part of his job.

COMO

There was a before and after that call. Patricia went back to the room with the yellow chintzes and woke up Aline, telling her that Doris needed to talk to her. She got up uneasy, because she knew that Doris would never bother her for trivialities, and even less knowing that she was spending her first hours at her father's lover's house. Something serious was coming down.

Pat led her into a room with frescoed ceilings and stuccoed doors. A desk with views of the lake and an amber-colored sofa completed the decor.

"It was my father's study. Important matters have been pondered in this room. His and mine," she confided to her before leaving her to herself.

Aline, for a moment, conjured up her father's shelter. The settings, although different, were impregnated with the same essence. She found herself in a magnificent study and, beyond the bay windows, gazed upon a century-old tree. The Ampurdán stone house was hidden beneath a fig tree, but its function was the same. The farmhouse and Villa Balbini continued to bear uncanny resemblances.

She put her thoughts aside and, worried, dialed the Lamberts' number. At the other end of the receiver, Doris, without preamble, informed her about the car accident in Palermo and Marco's death. Shock and pain in their full force washed over her. Aline avoided telling her that it might have been an intentional crash—given the kind of lifestyle her husband led—but the chaos she was immersed in prevented further elaboration.

"We lived apart," was the only thing she managed to say, her voice cracking with emotion.

Worried, she asked Doris who'd given the news. She wouldn't consent to see the Lamberts involved in this maelstrom.

"A lawyer, Michele Sassari, called me to let me know what had happened and asked for your address on behalf of his family. That's all I know. I'm sorry, even if I hadn't met your husband." This last sentence she said with the intention of stressing that she was aware of all that she'd hidden regarding her hasty marriage.

Stunned and bewildered, for she had always sensed that he would die in the most unexpected way and place, Aline began to understand why Erik was looking for her and why the Foreigner had been missing for days, as well as the drugs. Her deductions made her take stock of the situation. She didn't know Sassari but knew that Marco trusted him with his affairs. Having him come to Como would facilitate the answers. He would know firsthand the details of the incident and the fate of the merchandise. She also realized that if she sheltered him, she'd be sheltering the family, but her fear of Bürke outweighed what she felt for the organization.

She thought of Patricia and the seriousness of involving her in the feud. If she were to give a first impression regarding her personality, it would be that "the hardest part yet" concerned her. She reached the conclusion that the lawyer's visit would dispel her doubts and distance the Lamberts from the incident. So she agreed to let Doris tell him where she was.

The house and its surroundings' serenity provided her with an inner peace that allowed her to put the harrowing days out of her mind and recall the first night with the Foreigner in the Saudade and his forceful words when he asked her to marry him.

She had lain awake that night; the Costa Brava sea appeared lake-like. She recalled Doris' memorable words: "Lakes calm one down." Now, as she peered at the greenish waters of the one in front of her, Doris informed her of her husband's death. She went to the window and longed for the happy days spent by his side. She told herself that she would only cherish those which she now evoked.

Marco loved her so passionately that, at some point, she sensed that his end would have to do with her. She'd never know.

·ROME

Erik climbed the steps cursing Partana and wondering what could Salvatore's reason be for summoning him to the former's apartment, but what really gnawed at him was not knowing where the hell the drugs were. But if he wished to find out, he had no other choice but to show up. He didn't need to force the door, like last time when Aline appeared, a smart woman able to slip past his surveillance. He still couldn't figure out how she'd left the apartment.

On bursting into the apartment, he saw himself reflected in the oriental-looking mirror that framed the entrance. He had an impeccable tan from so much sailing and dressed with cosmopolitan elegance. Loafers had replaced the cowboy boots, and the blue shirt highlighted his broad shoulders. He settled back on the sofa and took off his sunglasses. The hitman received him with the same coldness with which he treated all others and didn't beat around the bush.

"Marco is dead." Having said this, he waited for his reaction without moving a muscle on his face.

"Dead?" Erik asked in disbelief, thinking that he was playing a joke on him; or, worse, that he was plotting something macabre.

"His car skidded in the curves of Bellocampo. But let's get to the point. What are you interested in?" Salvatore continued. "I have the goods. I know you must get it to the boss of the sailboat Gull."

"How do I know you're not lying?" Erik rebutted, wary of falling into a trap.

"You can call Luca, and he'll confirm it, although it appears we're without a phone…"

Erik flinched. He knew that the hitman was a man of few words and forceful actions. There was nothing to be gained by opposing him. His client had given him an ultimatum.

Deliberating the matter, he heard Salvatore's monotonous but firm voice once more, who went on unfazed, "I have instructions not to move from here till I have proof that Marco's wife is alive. If apart from cutting the wires, you've done something else, it'll be your problem."

The Norseman realized that the situation was out of his control and broke out in a cold sweat, which was unusual for him. He never thought that she was married to Partana. He now understood why they weren't making a move.

Salvatore made a face that left no room for doubt about his present and future intentions.

"They'll let me know when they find her."

Erik couldn't believe his ears. His life depended on Aline. Ever since the night in Ibiza when the Foreigner asked him for a special woman to forget her, at the same time that Ahmed desired her, he should've realized that something would happen. He simply followed both of their wishes, not knowing the girl's identity. And as if this wasn't enough, now he had to wait for them to find her so as not to die.

He got up and took a few steps to the Buddha statues that framed the dining room and leaned against one of them, seized by an attack that one might define as vertigo or panic.

"Very well," he said, "but I warn you, if they don't find her fast, the Dutch will kill us."

"They'll kill you," the hitman clarified, unfazed. "I'm going to prepare spaghetti. I'm hungry. Don't leave the apartment." And he headed toward the kitchen as if it were his own.

Erik was aware that Sicilians liked to eat while waiting for the living and before gathering the dead. Salvatore had his men come upstairs to splice the wires. It went without saying that Erik wasn't going to eat pasta.

COMO

Aline, leaning against the bay window facing the lake, brooded. The blow of Marco's death hit her at the height of uncertainty, although she wouldn't forgive him for involving her in his dirty business dealings. He took advantage of her inexperience and seduced her till he got her. In spite of it all, he made her very happy for a while and saved her estate in the blink of an eye.

She had lost track of the time that had elapsed since Doris' call, but when Pat entered the room, Aline, on seeing her, refused to lie to her. And, as if the two took it for granted that they would not avoid a dialogue that they'd been waiting to have for years, settled on the sofa. Aline, aware that she was not talking to a stranger, began to open up and begged that none of her confidences reach the Lamberts. Pat promised, and as she related her story, she felt that even though it was her life, it seemed like someone else's.

Aline did not omit anything from her first encounter with Marco: The first months believing she was happy, the discovery of his true identity, and her work in Renzo's atelier with its unexpected consequences. She continued narrating the sudden disappearance and death of her husband and Erik's threats when he was looking for the stash, to her escape to Villa Balbini, fleeing from Bürke, and her terrible fear of being killed. She felt it necessary to warn her that a lawyer for the Santacroces would be showing up at her house. And neither did she elude the painful subject of having consciously pushed her away and that it was her dread that prompted her to follow her father's advice and show up at her villa.

"I guess you weren't interested in meeting me," Patricia stated, giving the impression that everything else, including the mafia, was unimportant.

"I never wanted to, but today I regret it. My father suggested it, and when I refused, he didn't insist. Throughout my adolescence, I didn't want to share him with anyone. I pretended to be the only one in his life."

She revealed how she found out about their romance, crouched at the top of the fig tree, the hiding place, her ultimate secret. Now she didn't mind sharing it with Pat since it was part of that past.

"What he wanted has occurred. The rest will fall into place." She sighed and, with an endearing gesture, took her hand.

Aline thought that perhaps Pat hadn't grasped the scope of the Foreigner's affairs, but a few days later, and as their trust grew, she recognized her innate strength and wisdom before the grueling situations that shape one's life. She then understood why her father had directed her to Villa Balbini. Doris wouldn't have been able to bear the stress or the Norseman's threats. Pat, on the other hand, would be capable of withstanding them with perfect aplomb. She conveyed a sense of fortitude that was intimidating.

As she listened to her talk about her origins, she deduced that that mixture of self-control and strength came from her mother, the daughter of prosperous English bankers who fell in love with the estate and bought it but were forced to return to England due to war. Once it was over, they returned to Italy to sadly find Villa Balbini in ruins. Vandals and passing soldiers left it in a state that required several years of extensive restoration. Her father, the Neapolitan count Massimo Di Borgo, educated, elegant and intelligent, was a great art collector and patron of the arts. He had a direct relationship with the Italian and Spanish nobility in Naples and had an important heritage that he increased with successful purchases and financial operations, all thanks to his social skills and lasting friendships.

The days rolled by. In the evening, when it cooled down, Pat and Aline walked through the gardens. The latter listened to the descriptions of her father's lover about real stories and legends regarding the Villa, while she feared Sassari's imminent arrival and his dubious explanations. Every night they talked about Henry and exchanged their own life lessons by his side. Aline enjoyed them, and Pat reaffirmed her belief that her relationship with Henry had followed the course that was their lot to live.

The house had two small jetties. One extended toward the water between some trees, with an easy access ladder for bathing. The other was used to enter the lake with motor or rowing boats. Patricia suggested going out one morning to row. The waters were as calm as a mirror.

"Did you row with your father?" Aline asked when the boat's roll recalled her nights of fishing and the Costa Brava sea crashing against the rocks.

"Of course, when the weather was good, we'd go out every day." And, without her asking, she shed light on how her father influenced her bond with Henry. "You know, Aline, I adored Massimo," —she called her father by his name— "and I would've had a hard time accepting that he remarry. I knew Betsy's indifference toward you, and I understood that it was essential for you two to stick together. I acted accordingly. Henry was absorbed by his work, and I had already lived long enough to accept a fragmented relationship. I'd say that's the best word to define it. Besides, taking care of the art collection and family heirlooms took up the rest of my time when he wasn't around." She finished the sentence looking into infinity, as if searching in that immensity for the men who had meant so much in her life.

Aline answered that misfortunes had to happen for her to be there and finally understand her altruism.

"I know." And, with sudden emotion, confessed, "I spent my youth with Massimo. We were constantly traveling...I was imbued with his culture. We were happy. When he died, I thought I wouldn't be able to overcome his loss; you, of all people, will know what I mean."

Aline understood, then and there, that they were united by feelings and circumstances more similar than she could have fathomed.

"It was in a plane crash in Croydon, south of London. It was snowing that day, and the airport was covered in low clouds and fog. The plane skidded sideways and crashed into another. He was traveling to Pretoria to visit my husband and me."

"You lived in Pretoria?" It seemed to her a continent so far from Como that it was disconcerting.

"My husband was the Italian ambassador in that country...of jacarandas. But that is another story."

That phrase, which prevented the dialogue from moving forward, marked the return to the villa.

ROME

When Salvatore received Michele's call confirming that Aline was alive and knew her whereabouts, the former took a few seconds to inform Erik, who was pacing the apartment like a caged lion.

"They've given the go-ahead." And unblinking added, "I have instructions to go with you to the island and check the delivery together." He concluded that this seemed to be an issue between Partana and Bürke that the Don wanted wrapped up.

The Norseman, incredulous, was on the verge of hitting him. He quickly caught himself. Nobody gave him orders, but he was dealing with one of the most expeditious men he'd ever met, and he knew quite a few. For some reason that he couldn't figure out, Salvatore was two steps ahead and had the dope. There was no other choice than to put up with him. He clenched his teeth till he hurt himself. Without the slightest idea where the stash was and with that Sicilian coercing him, he reflected. Since setting foot in the apartment, he had done nothing but wait, threatened with death by the Dutch and the mafia.

Now, having to carry on with this hateful fellow made him strangely wary. First, he had hoped in vain that Marco would show signs of life. It was a business between them, and it wasn't wise to get the organization involved. Afterward, he ran into Aline and assumed that she'd know where the hell he was.

He went up to the liquor cabinet and drank half a bottle of whiskey in the blink of an eye. Drinking alcohol helped him calm down, but he did so thinking about where on earth that damned woman causing so many headaches was.

When they landed in Ibiza, the pleasant temperature was a far cry from the mugginess of the summer months. Salvatore was always intrigued by the island's contrasts, the hippies, and its mystical surroundings. He knew a few farms hidden in the countryside which were used as hideaways for criminals who wished to remain anonymous. They all enjoyed the freedom that the island offered. The local's lack of interest in the vicissitudes that took place on their land struck him from the very first day he set foot on it.

Erik led him directly to his black Range Rover with the tinted windows, which he always left in the exterior parking lot. He glanced at the man sitting next to him as he started the engine. Either he trusted him, or he'd bit the dust. They drove to the port in dead silence, and there boarded Bürke's yacht, who relived the fateful night in which Aline began to complicate his life. He'd seen her for the first time at his country house. She'd suddenly showed up. Who knows why; nobody expected her. On the Ishtar, Ahmed, with unusual tenacity, wanted to possess her. He would've given her the diamond he lent her and much more, but Marco brought the wrong girl aboard the yacht. Now he was dead without having made the delivery, and he'd lost control of the situation when, not knowing that it was his wife, he had threatened to kill her. The Sicilians would hardly forget that detail.

They entered the boat's saloon, and Salvatore sprawled out on the sofa and put his bare feet on the table.

Then he spoke, in that tone of voice that he managed to drive Erik up the wall, "You'll have to contact the Dutchman and let him know that the delivery will be made at eight PM in Cala Truja. The coast guards have been bought off, so there shouldn't be any hitches. They're waiting for you." He paused and added, "Send the family's cut to the usual place."

"The usual place" was an account of one of the companies that Sassari had set up on a Caribbean island. In it, Bürke deposited the share that corresponded to the profits obtained through Partana's contacts.

Erik swallowed the fear that this rough character instilled in him. He had nothing to do with Marco, who, while attending meetings with powerful people, flew first class and checked himself in the finest hotel of Costa Smeralda. His people took care of the dirty work.

Now, due to the circumstances, neither of them trusted the other. Salvatore controlled him, and he had to do the same with the drugs. With a sarcastic smile, he said, "By the way, since you're going to have to wait for me, the liquor cabinet has plenty of alcohol. And if you're hungry, the crew has prepared food. I trust you'll enjoy my hospitality."

Once he reached his cabin, he got out of his elegant suit and put on a pair of jeans, a T-shirt, and his usual boots, while he cursed the damn day that Marco tempted him with this affair. The whirlwind in which he was caught up had forced him to neglect his own interests. His boss, Wasyl Yurchenko, was waiting for him in Munich for a crucial meeting, and delaying this appointment was out of the question.

He swore in German and left the boat. Exasperated, he drove to San Antonio, the town where the Dutch were waiting for him, hoping not to be ambushed. The island, as usual, basked in its gentle daily sway.

Salvatore went out on deck. He took a look at the city walls, thinking that they must've been essential in past skirmishes. A shame, he thought, that they were no longer built. He was fascinated by the old town hidden behind them…He had a hard time following the instructions that Sassari had given. He was like a fish out of water in such a luxurious boat. He was in his element during the slaughtering season or in the underworld. Come to think of it, between tequila and tequila, if Marco's wife had remained hidden, his host would already be dead.

It was late in the afternoon when Erik got back to the boat. He and Salvatore got into a zodiac and slowly headed for Es Vedrá, where the sailboat was anchored. Paul waited anxiously, but given what had been paid and agreed upon, he had no other choice than to do so without protest. Once on board, they went down to the hold and took out the drugs that were hidden in a false bottom. Erik went through the stash, which he didn't usually do. In fact, he didn't usually go on deliveries. Thinking it through, what for Marco must've been a game, for him, was a major risk. They could still break his neck, but Partana always managed to convince him. However, since he was dead, he now had to deal with his henchmen, and not only were they aware of where the stash was, but they also gave him orders. It was absurd.

Paul took the sealed packets containing the white powder and put them into the rubber sacks he used to store his diving suits. As he started the sailboat's engines, he explained that he'd be approaching within a kilometer of the small rocky cove. The isle was left behind, and only the peculiar sound of the waters crashing against the bow of the ship could be heard. On reaching the established point, Paul threw the bundles onto a launch and, from it, accompanied by an attractive blonde, headed for Cala Truja. Salvatore and Erik followed the swift operation with powerful binoculars as the Dutch removed the bales. The Sicilian thought that if he hurried, he would arrive in time to catch the last flight to the peninsula and shed the bad omens that assailed him every time he looked at Bürke. The latter, fed up, decided that he needed a woman to relax before his date with Yurchenko. The night was upon them.

COMO

The lawyer, Sassari, stopped the car at the entrance to Villa Balbini. He took a few steps to the wrought iron gate. He pushed it; it was open. He observed the proud beauty of the place and speculated on the ties that bound Aline with the Villa's owners.

He was there for one sole purpose: To put on record what Marco's last wishes were, resolve all financial matters without the interference of lawyers on the part of the former's wife, and make sure that she'd keep silent. These were his thoughts whilst, skirting the pond, he entered the cypress-line path that led to the mansion.

The housekeeper escorted him through several sumptuous salons to a cozy sitting room with a pleasant fireplace in the middle. He imagined the owners spending their leisure time there.

It wasn't long before Aline appeared. He realized that she had nothing in common with the voluptuous Sicilian women, beautiful and shy, or at least that is how they portrayed themselves. Her slim, graceful silhouette was swan-like in its grace. The beautiful features of her face made Sassari think of the Madonnas of his native land, one of the many to whom his wife entrusted herself when the hard times hit. It was no wonder Partana fell head over heels for her.

Once the introductions were made, Aline told him that she'd rather walk as they talked, and they headed for the garden. She was quick to ask how he'd gotten the Lamberts' phone number.

"It wasn't hard. Marco told me that you'd lived with them in Paris."

He made it clear that he first tried, unsuccessfully, to get a hold of her as soon as the accident occurred and then told her what had happened; but omitted everything else. Aline listened, adopting a reserved attitude that concealed a sense of forewarning.

"You were his lawyer," and without showing her anxiety, went on, "and we'd separated. I was waiting for a call from him…"

"That's no longer important," Sassari declared, as if he were part of a court of justice. "The main thing is what he wanted and arranged so that your future would be assured." He immediately strove to give a professional note to his arrangements. "The apartment on Via in Lucina will have to be vacated. I've opened an account to your name at a bank in Zurich" he handed her a business card, "you just have to contact this person. There is a considerable sum. You must move on and forget."

Aline realized that she was being given an order but didn't for one minute doubt that this was the most sensible thing to do. She mentally went over the organization's way of operating. Those in power were aware of the slightest movement. No one did anything on their own initiative. Sassari must have known, in detail, what had happened, but Aline didn't dare throw in his face that he must be aware of the facts. Marco taught her certain rules; following them to the letter was her own defense. He wouldn't have left her unprotected, and in business, he kept his promises. She couldn't figure out what hidden forces had triggered that error.

She looked at the man with the questioning stare, and the bitterness vanished, giving way to the essence of the facts.

"I'm here because I'm running away from Bürke. He was beside himself and threatened me. He was looking for Marco and some merchandise. That's what he said."

"He won't bother you again," he answered categorically.

On hearing that, Aline assumed that the deal had gone through. She tried to be careful because Sicilian women didn't stick their noses in their men's affairs. She was convinced that the revelations the Foreigner had made to her were on purpose so that she'd distance herself from him. The family must not suspect this, not even vaguely. Saying the minimum was the most sensible thing to do.

"I want to make sure you'll follow my advice." He made an effort not to let his voice give away that he was pressuring her.

She looked at him as if wanting to roam his mind. Since she knew the criminal origin of the money, she rejected it but swore to him what he wanted to hear. Along with her words, a slight breeze rustled the trees' leaves and stirred them on the ground.

Aline relived her conversations with Patricia; she was sure that the latter would keep it to herself. Once the promise was made, the years with the Foreigner had died along with it.

Michele realized why that girl had married the Don's godson. He could charm women and captivate people, no matter their background. The truth was that he'd concealed his marriage for a long time. They were all convinced that he'd follow tradition and marry a Sicilian, a woman accustomed to the island's way of life, but no one imagined that he'd do as he did.

Putting his speculations aside, Michele said the only thing he could tell her was, "Your husband was deeply in love with you."

Michele was eager to get back to Palermo right away, to his office on Via della Libertà, to his daily routine. That story was unusual, and the worst thing was that he sensed that it had just begun.

Aline watched him move away. Without a choice, he had tried to transmit to her a strength that he lacked. Too many unknowns lay in wait.

She felt the late afternoon's dampness cling to her skin and looked around her. It seemed as if there was no other place on the planet where she could feel as protected as in Villa Balbini, and she reached the conclusion that there was no other choice than to continue deceiving everyone except Patricia.

At least with her, she didn't need to pretend.

CHAPTER 8

ROME

Haim Weiss was having a coffee first thing in the morning on the terrace of the bar *I Tre Scalini* in Piazza Navona. It was early enough for the tourists to start coming out of their hotels and late enough for the Romans to have their second ristretto before heading for the office.

He had been assigned to the Eternal City on a specific mission. Rome had become a hotbed for Middle East terrorists seeking information, and arms dealers wanted reliable customers. Behind him was his brilliant career in physics and his job at a French multinational. Nothing suggested that he'd end up becoming a highly regarded officer of the Mossad's special services; that is, a *Katsa*. His father always hid his work for the Mossad behind his post at the embassy, but Haim was not approached from that angle. The unexpected offer was made to him by a well-known Jewish publisher and recruiter one night while they were having dinner at the latter's house. He accepted without a second thought. He was not moved by money but by attachment to his country and its ideals.

The training lasted three years. He reminisced about the extremely violent interrogations he had been subjected to, which alternated with harsh desert survival training. After the grueling process, his cunning increased beyond imagination. Once he became an expert sniper, he learned to decipher messages to achieve objectives and acquired the ability to improvise on the fly. Cold blood prevailed over all things, for his first mistake could be his last. He had several passports and spoke perfect French, English, Hebrew, and Arabic. He had a photographic memory, something that was essential when contrasting plans and vital information for the success of the missions entrusted by the Agency.

His main mission was to locate the enemy and gather the necessary information so as to eliminate him. Haim had two agents who'd infiltrated the city's Arab community for the past several months, tracking various arms dealers. The Shin Bet, Israel's internal security agency, tasked with neutralizing terrorist organizations within the country and which coordinated with him and his team, was in charge of dismantling the cargo before it fell into their hands.

Someone brushed his shoulder, and his senses went on alert.

"Haim?"

He raised his head and immediately recognized her. He was struck by Aline's appearance, the opposite of the last time they'd seen each other four long years earlier. She had traded her helpless air for a seductive one. A tight sweater and a straight skirt outlined a silhouette that seemed perfect. Running into her in the early hours of the morning in the Eternal City was something most unexpected. Aline had traveled from Como to Rome to solve tedious and inevitable paperwork.

"What are you doing here?" he asked, perplexed, hugging her tightly.

As he held her in his arms, he recalled how hard it had been for him to get over her sudden departure from Paris. Shortly thereafter, the Lamberts, worried, confirmed that she'd married an Italian, whose only reference was his comfortable economic position. Hurt by her silence, he'd visit Doris often to seek consolation, as well as to try and get some news; but he soon discovered that Doris hardly knew much more about Aline's new life. Given the whirlwind in which he soon found himself, and knowing that if he went looking for her, he'd be forced to pretend made him desist, but he still could not understand why she'd behaved in such a manner, not at all in keeping with the girl with whom he'd shared adventures and secrets. With his newly-acquired skill, he sensed that the two were hiding something, and for that reason, they had both avoided contact.

Aline, amazed at her friend's change, sat down at the table and gazed at Haim. His faded freckles were no longer those that in the past had invaded his skin, which had now lost its paleness. His body had the build of an athlete, as if he'd been trained to be one. He gave off an absolute firmness in his every gesture. She figured he'd still have that particular way of being, which was the pillar that helped her overcome the biggest obstacle she'd ever faced.

She ordered a cappuccino, hoping that the next few seconds would allow her to come up with a reason that would justify her incomprehensible behavior, but she didn't find one. Hoping he wouldn't hold a grudge, she told him about Marco's death.

"We were separated," she clarified.

"I'm sorry." And without beating around the bush, despite knowing that he would open an old wound, he asked, "Is there something you can't tell me?"

Haim fell silent, wondering what kind of predicament she'd been in. He was thankful for the cover that masked his true identity; had she known, Aline wouldn't have uttered the last sentence, and he wouldn't have decided to dwell on her past. He planned to deal with that unknown in the following hours. He sensed her guilt, and it was difficult to discern what had happened. She had clearly lost the spontaneity that characterized her along the way.

"Now that you know, I want to tell you how much I've missed you." And, with a touch of nostalgia, Aline carried on, "I always carry with me those words that you said during one of our walks in the *Bois de Boulogne*."

"What words?"

"You assured me that my father's soul would protect me because he was a Jew. I wanted to believe you, but I've often felt that that protection has failed me."

"Don't doubt it. And think that there is always an alternative. Always," he reaffirmed.

"I wish we hadn't drifted apart. I kept going because your convictions swept me along," Aline replied, realizing that they were as strong as ever.

"Then fight; there is a reason why you're in this world. Your father taught you how to do so, not because there was any guarantee of success, but because fighting itself is the only way to continue to have faith in life."

"And what are you doing here?" she asked; and kept to herself the wise advice he had given her.

Weiss told her bluntly about the Mossad-orchestrated scenario that he used as a cover. He worked as a consultant in Olma, an Italian machinery company in which he was in charge of supervising the development of a new product. He lived in an aparthotel. In any event, he stressed the fact that in no more than a month, he'd be back in France.

Aline believed him without the least hint of suspicion when he offered to accompany her to collect her belongings from the apartment where she had lived with her husband. What she was far from foreseeing is that Haim would soon have the detailed file on the Santacroce in his possession and learn everything, to the very last detail of Partana's life.

Then she wrote Pat's address in Rome on a napkin and stated, "It's a friend's house. I live there."

He put it in his pocket, paid the bill, and gave her his phone number, although it was actually the number of a *sayan*, a volunteer Jewish collaborator of the Mossad who answered his calls.

"Excuse me, but they're waiting for me. I'll pick you up at six tomorrow," Haim said and then whispered in her ear, "Trust yourself."

And disappeared in one of the many alleys that converged on the square. He did not want to talk to her about his marriage or about his wife, who died in a terrorist attack in Jerusalem. The bomb blast hit her as she was leaving work at the hospital, causing her injuries that, in spite of doctors' efforts who treated her, she was unable to overcome. He would never be able to reveal his true profession or his marriage with Hanna. It would give rise to a number of questions that he was forbidden to answer.

Aline remained pensive for a while, watching the water flow from the square's fountain. Knowing that Haim would accompany her to her apartment from which she'd escaped Bürke's clutches reassured her. Finding her friend, she thought, would have something to do with one of those coincidences that change, straighten, or destroy a person. She had the feeling that this coincidence came from beyond.

Three days later, Guido Moretti, a close friend of Patricia's and Henry Asher in his day, picked up Aline at the Milan airport, for he too was spending a few nights at the villa. He had business affairs to attend to in Como. Pat was in the habit of inviting her friends to the villa, where she'd welcome them and, over gin and tonics, talk till late into the night. The idea of company appealed to Aline, and she knew the idyllic setting would bring much-needed serenity. She felt threatened in Rome, saw danger at every corner, and the city was a reminder of her most recent past. The phrase that Haim uttered on saying goodbye: "Think things through, I beg you. If you need me, call me," after collecting the essentials from her apartment, further enhanced her fears. The vicissitudes were not over.

She had no difficulty spotting Guido when he crossed the gate after he'd picked up his luggage. Of medium height, he wore a plaid blazer and sweatpants, an outfit that made him stand out among the serious businessmen who landed at Linate Airport early in the morning. His shock of white hair highlighted the tanned skin. According to Pat's description, he was human, a fighter, and felt very Roman. From the terrace of his attic, near Castel Sant'Angelo, Guido watched the waters of the Tiber go by. His work at the company, a leader in the distribution of fabrics, frequently took him to Como, where he'd stop over at Villa Baldini to spend the night.

This time around, the drive's last hour and a half to the villa had nothing to do with Aline's previous harrowing journey, when she fled Bürke, and in which there had been a terrifying fog-laden final stretch. Guido gave off enthusiasm which she badly needed. He asked the precise questions in order for her to confess to her failed marriage and Marco's subsequent death. Then he, in an effort to snatch her out of her despondency and free her from further explanations, took the initiative and told her about his work, his life, and his friendship with Henry. He revealed that it was at Villa Balbini that he met him and that, although different from one another, they had more in common than met the eye.

The Moretti family, who were Jewish, were forced to flee as soon as the Italian government, in the midst of war, introduced anti-Semitic laws. They immigrated to the United States. His relatives took them in, and he began to work in the chain of clothing stores that they managed in New York. A decade later, already in the fifties, when his son Michael turned twelve, he returned to Italy a widower. His wife, like grandmother Katinka, was unable to endure the grief of having left the country and her friends in such circumstances.

Aline reminisced about her family's flight while listening to him, and, something that had never happened before with anyone, she told him about her father and her uprooting since his death, about grandfather Samuel, and about offering prayers in the Parisian synagogue. When they arrived at their destination, she felt as if she'd known him forever.

Patricia received them while cutting flowers in the garden, which ended up as a centerpiece under the pergola where the convivial lunch took place. She apologized to both of them for her busy schedule, but she'd lent some paintings from the valuable collection for an important exhibition in Venice, which meant a never-ending amount of paperwork that she had to work out with her secretary. Also, dealing with the press, which was coming to photograph the villa and her works of art, was all part of certain unavoidable obligations.

"Well, I'm expected at several companies," Guido announced so that Pat wouldn't have to worry about him. "I have to choose silks for my American clients. Their tastes are so different from ours that it takes me entire afternoons to come up with what they're looking for." He finished the sentence with a gesture of despair.

Aline looked at him with interest. She was ignorant of that great little world of silk shops and asked if she could accompany him. Moreover, she was excited to do so, accompanied by a friend of her father's.

In the following days, Pat spent her time checking the packaging of paintings, selecting photos, and dealing with journalists, and meanwhile, they went looking for prints which Aline ended up choosing. Between Jacquard and Jacquard, Guido learned that she'd worked for Pisani. He was not at all surprised because her competence and good taste were obvious. Since Renzo's excesses were an open secret, he concluded that the couturier surrounded himself with very effective people capable of taking the initiative when he was walking on thin ice. It was obvious that she was part of that group. The creator's business moved too much money for it to be at the mercy of his excesses.

On a warm midday, while eating a delicious polenta with fish at La Trattoria del Vapore in Cernobbio, near Como, Guido asked why she no longer was at the atelier.

"I didn't get along with Carla," Aline replied curtly.

He figured that, for some reason, talking about it was taboo. They were in no hurry, so they carried on chatting till they ended up alone in the small restaurant. Aline shared her doubts regarding her future without telling him the truth. Her years with Marco had left her empty and exhausted. Directing her life without having the slightest idea of how to go about doing it and where, was the dilemma.

When the light faded and the mists seemed eager to alter the landscape, they went down to the lakefront to wait for the *vaporetto* that would take them back to Como. Guido put his hands in his pockets and as if he sensed that something more than widowhood had disrupted Aline's life, said, "Some things are incomprehensible or seem so, but if you dig deeper, you'll find out why. I know so from experience."

And Aline, during those evenings, tried to do just that in the haven of peace that was Villa Balbini.

The SID (Italian Secret Service) colonel entered the Café Greco in Via Condotti and, as was his custom, sat with his back to the wall to keep an eye on the room. He ordered a Cinzano, and Weiss arrived shortly thereafter, with whom he used to exchange information and favors. Just like in roulette, the events on both sides didn't stop rotating at a frantic pace, which as professionals, they mastered. Weiss wanted to know everything about Marco Partana, and the colonel showed him some pages devoid of letterhead that described the Santacroces' activities.

"The worst thing was that Partana had contacts with high-ranking government officials. They went hand in hand, so to speak," he pointed out, scanning the surroundings and cautiously placing the reports on the table. "Strange thing is that he's died in an accident, and the family will have a hard time without him. He made fortunes for his people and those involved. Nobody will speak."

He took a few sips of vermouth and handed him some photos taken with a powerful lens. Marco could clearly be made out on the deck of the yacht owned by a major construction businessman.

"Friendships?" Haim asked.

"He had them spread out all over the world, in the Masonic lodge and in high society. Keep in mind that he studied at an elite university in Milan. On his ship, the Saudade, he sailed alone with the crew. After that, he did it with her, they liked the sea. From time to time, he sailed out with important people for business reasons and thus ensured, if need be, the necessary alibi. He did not deal in arms, but a certain Erik Bürke, who does, appears on the list of his acquaintances. He most likely provided him with contacts."

"What else is known about Bürke?"

"He works for Wasyl Yurchenko. He's in charge of his shipments. They call him the Norseman. He has an export-import company as a front, in the business district of EUR, in Rome. He doesn't usually stop in the city. He's constantly on the move. Where the arms go, he goes. His clients are of any ideology. As long as they pay, the rest is unimportant. We don't know what his future movements will be."

Haim deduced that, at some point, Aline must have found out about her husband's real business and, for safety's sake, kept quiet. She stayed away from the Lamberts so as not to have to lie to them.

"And his wife?" he asked as if he'd never seen her.

"She appeared out of the blue. Spanish. Unconnected to the case."

"I owe you one," Haim replied, frowning and finishing his coffee.

He'd just checkmated the mysterious disappearance of her friend.

Guido jumped at the chance and contacted his friends in the fashion world, who were quick to inform him of Aline's impeccable work at Renzo's atelier. Just as he'd thought, she'd be of great value to the Americans who were lost in everything except the number of dollars they handled.

Under the pergola of Villa Balbini, during one of their pleasant meals, he presented his idea to her. It wouldn't be difficult to convince one of the main shareholders of Bloomingdale's in New York to sign an agreement for Aline to collaborate on the creative side and act as a consultant. The two women exchanged glances, certain that they were thinking the same thing. That proposal solved the main problem: She'd move away from the ominous environment and start working.

"Well," Guido spoke, "I figure that if you don't contradict me, you're in agreement. I'll find him. He's on holiday in the Côte d'Azur, along with one of his associates. They'll be staying at the Hotel Negresco; I'll arrange a meeting with him." He finished drinking his liquor, got up, and went inside to make the call.

Pat, who understood Henry's daughter's fear of her present situation, saw in her face the uncertainty that hadn't faded since the day she spoke to Michele Sassari. She assured her that things would go back to normal. Although deep down, she wasn't too sure herself. She crossed her fingers, hoping there would be no more surprises.

The drive to Nice was pleasant and relaxed. Aline and Guido had become close, to the point where they talked casually about everything except Marco. He thought that this rejection of hers was a consequence of Aline's state of mind and ended by acknowledging that it be best not to insist, just as he did not dare ask why it took her so long to come near the Villa. She must've had her reasons. Patricia always held out hope of meeting her much sooner.

They were traveling in an Alfa Romeo convertible. It was the start of summer. Aline buttoned up her linen blazer and asked Guido to tell her about Pat's husband.

"Ever since the day we shared confidences, I was left with a desire to know…"

"If you want to know the truth, I met her as a widow, and she spoke little about him, but one afternoon when we were walking through the villa's gardens, I saw the proteas and some typical South African plants in a greenhouse and, curious, I asked. She confessed that, despite the misfortunes experienced in Pretoria, she wanted to surround herself with the same vegetation that hemmed the embassy in the suburb of Arcadia. She then talked about her husband. She never mentioned him by name, just called him the Ambassador. He was Milanese, and the diplomatic career marked his destiny and completely absorbed him. He met Pat at a reception in Rome, and from that moment on, they were never apart. He was ambassador in several countries before being posted to South Africa, a country that captivated them." Guido slowed down and added, "One day, they traveled with some friends to the Kruger National Park in Limpopo. Patricia is adventurous and has never been intimidated by anything. The trip, although long, was worth it. Seeing the landscapes and the species of wild animals that populated it was a unique experience. On the way back, the ambassador fell ill with malaria, and his condition worsened. That was the end."

Overwhelmed, Aline asked, "How did she recover from this tragedy?"

"A few years went by, and I thought she wouldn't come out of her state of apathy; until Henry showed up. She regained her smile and resumed with strength and determination the responsibilities that having an art collection like hers implies. She even went back to rowing in the lake, something that she'd stopped doing, like so many other things."

Aline longed to relive Pat's experience with her father: That someone someday would give her the opportunity to love once again. She was sure that Guido remembered with nostalgia the years he had just finished narrating.

Upon arriving at Ventimiglia, on the border with France, instead of continuing along the fast highway, they made their way along the sea in silence.

The *belle époque* style building that housed the Hotel Negresco was the ideal place to meet with the Americans. There was art in every nook and corner. Aline glanced around her room, embellished with deco furnishings, bearing no resemblance to the one on the above floor, in Louis XIII style. There, Guido chose to rest and do some work. They opted to have dinner at Le Chantecler restaurant, so she decided that a long walk would do her good. In the hall, a uniformed doorman opened the door for her. She headed for the port, as he suggested. On coming out into the street, she paused with intuitive caution. She had been doing so ever since Bürke showed up at the apartment; since his unexpected visit, she felt that her nerves were failing her. She gazed at the sea, calm in the late afternoon, at the wealthy tourists lined up on deckchairs on the beach, and at the row of tall palm trees that seemed to be pointing the direction to follow. She hardly knew that her stay in Nice would alter her future, just like the day when her rowboat drifted off the Costa Brava.

On reaching the harbor, she looked up at the yachts and felt a pang of remembrance; the Saudade was a distant memory, the smell of the sea, her nights of lovemaking with Marco, and the anxiety from the day she discovered the stash of drugs.

Suddenly, a voice calling her from the deck of one of the yachts brought her out of her daydreaming. A man who radiated elegance, strength, and intelligence—and whom she would've paid not to see again—asked her aboard and wouldn't take no for an answer. Ahmed Rahhal sent a crewman to escort her to him. On seeing her, he had to admit to himself that he was used to getting the women he desired, but Aline had become a fixation. He would not let her discern the attraction that couldn't be quashed, that pursued him ever since he lay eyes on her. If she were to become his, he wanted her to feel the same way but thought that that would be difficult. He fixed his gaze on the stranger, hoping that she'd cease to be. He noticed her honey-colored skin and her almond-shaped eyes. She looked like a Lebanese.

"I want to talk to you. It's my duty to apologize," he said, inviting her to enter the saloon, still not sure she'd accept.

Aline hesitated for a few seconds but didn't object, though reliving the night aboard the Ishtar brought back bad memories.

They settled into the long sofas that were part of the elegant setting. Neutral tones and magnificent wood furniture predominated. The relief decorations on the walls with middle-eastern motifs gave an unusual brushstroke to the entire saloon. Ahmed had tea served. Aline was able to scrutinize him, something that did not occur on that gloomy night on the yacht's bow. His broad forehead, one might say powerful, was furrowed with fine lines, the same ones that appeared at the corner of his lips and denoted strength of character. His short black hair had some gray. He must've been in his forties. A magnetic aura endowed him with a charismatic personality. He kept looking at her, and Aline felt the intensity of his person focused on her in a special way. With poise and without trying to justify his behavior, Ahmed stated what he thought.

"I was unaware that you were married to Marco Partana."

Aline interrupted him. "Had you known, would you have not made the proposition?" she asked, remembering how Marco told her that Rahhal would never take a friend's wife, even less so if he were in business with him.

"Never," he cut her short, thinking how he'd been mistaken on seeing her come on board with the Norseman. "Bürke didn't tell me who you were."

"I was unaware," she answered tensely and thought it was no use holding his behavior against him, certain that she'd never see him again.

"I know your husband has passed away, and I'm sorry." And, with the temperance with which the Arabs assume adverse events, he declared, "It was written in his destiny."

"I don't believe in destiny. Each one of us builds it step by step. How did you find out?"

"It doesn't matter. Bad news flies, and it came along with the fact that you were his wife," and he uttered some unexpected words. "You can't trust life, Aline. You must live the moment because you have no control over it. What God giveth, God takes away. It's not in your hands."

That phrase reminded him not of Partana but of her father. It summed up the philosophy that he applied daily: Live each moment as if it were the last.

"There's something I need to know. What is your relationship with Erik?" On naming him, he noted the disgust produced on Aline's face.

"I met him a few hours before dinner that night. Marco was staying at his farm, and I arrived unexpectedly, but I don't wish to talk about him. I am here, and you've clarified a situation that was most unpleasant."

The skirt covered her legs, and a wide belt highlighted her waist. Her blouse revealed a pendant that caught Ahmed's attention, and he asked to see it. When he had it in the palm of his hand, he opened it and said, "It's an Arab amulet, the *ayat-al-kursi*. If you wear it, you will always enjoy protection. Where did you get it?"

"A kid, Ali, gave it to me in Paris."

Ahmed wanted to know more, and she had the impression of reliving the night aboard the Ishtar when he asked her what she was looking for in the stars. He wouldn't give up trying until he knew. It seemed to Aline that she was experiencing a unique situation and, perhaps because of this, told him how she almost perished under the wheels of a car to protect Ali.

"Why did you do it?" he asked, surprised, as if for a split second he doubted her emotions.

"My father instilled in me beliefs that I have always tried to live up to. For a Jew to save a life is to save the world."

"For the Arabs, too, although I've never been in that situation. What else did he teach you besides bravery?"

"To fail and start over again. That has been, in my worst moments, an unconditional help."

"We're different. I was raised to obey and not fail, but with my father's help, I've developed the ability to make the impossible possible. Now tell me, what were you doing in Paris?"

Aline wondered what could it possibly matter to him what she might be doing on the Av. des Sycomores…However, in a sudden burst of nostalgia, she told him the reason for her presence in the city.

The amulet returned to her hands through those of Ahmed, who, on making the gesture, left them for a few seconds between hers, thoughtful.

"I've answered your questions. Now you must answer mine. I don't think you always live on luxury yachts," Aline said.

"I am Lebanese, and my home is in Ras Beirut." And suspecting that she was in no hurry to end the conversation, he elaborated, explaining his activities. "My business interests range from construction to exports to a number of countries. I also own a stable. I am passionate about horses. I ride as much as I can because it gives me a feeling of absolute freedom."

He told her how proud Arabs were of their steeds, which were distinguished by their thick manes and short dorsal spines, which made it easier for them to traverse rough terrain. He also spoke to her about the desert and assured her that when assailed by doubts, he'd penetrate it to meditate before making any important decision.

"Something that you Jews also usually do," he stated.

Aline, who had never set foot in one, felt that Haim had forgotten to mention something important to her. Now, listening to Ahmed talk about the wild landscapes, she thought that there was no other space in the universe that could be so close to God.

His musings were interrupted by a crew member who appeared in the room. He went up to Rahhal and informed him that, according to the weather report, a storm was on its way, and it would be impossible to follow the intended route to Corsica. If they wanted to set sail in a few hours, it was essential to change the travel plan.

"Sorry," he apologized. "The boat belongs to Georges Haleemi, my cousin, and he's absent. I have to give instructions to the captain."

Aline was left alone. She faintly felt the smell of iodine and saltpeter. She stroked the amulet. Not even she herself knew what prompted her to hang it around her neck that day. It had been kept in a little box for years. That action, unconscious, had just given rise to talk about her years in Paris. Pure longing, she thought to herself.

The minutes seemed eternal. It was getting dark. Nervous, she stood up and walked the short distance from the large saloon to a smaller one. She glanced around and, turning back, her attention was caught by a jumble of papers, written in Arabic, sticking out from an open briefcase lying on a table. She drew near with a certain apprehension. At the top of one of them, Partana's name appeared. Her sixth sense alerted her. She was unable to hold back. Just as she reached for it, with an anxiety that was paralyzing, she heard and saw, out of the corner of her eye, Ahmed burst back into the room.

With a quick gesture and feigning normalcy, she managed to stick it in her bag. She gasped, thinking what would happen if someone were to notice that it'd gone missing and wanted it back. She tried not to lose her composure and informed Ahmed that they were waiting for her. She was impatient to leave the boat and pretty much ignored his wish to know what she was doing in Nice. At the foot of the ladder, a friendly, inscrutable, and protective Rahhal held out his hand, making it clear that they would meet again.

With deep seriousness, he stated, "There is an Arabic proverb that says: 'The past has fled, what you hope for is absent, but the present is yours.' You must seize it."

Aline didn't answer. The shock that overwhelmed her didn't seem to dissipate. She was still aboard the Sapphire, surrounded by a Lebanese crew who, at the slightest order, would pounce on her. She had sworn to forget the Foreigner, but at every step, she seemed to stumble upon him, as if Marco didn't want to disappear.

She let go of the Arab's hand just as Georges was climbing the ladder where they were saying goodbye. He was a young man who conveyed the frenetic pace of the West, as if the parsimony of the East was not his thing. He exchanged a few words with his cousin, mixing several languages. Before hurrying into the yacht, he greeted her with polite coldness. Not even when stepping on land did Aline feel safe.

The Boulevard des Anglais seemed endless. She calmed down on catching a glimpse of the hotel's pink dome. Guido was waiting for her at the entrance.

During the meeting with the Americans, real financial sharks, Aline missed Renzo. It was impossible to make them understand that blue could have as many shades as the skies that surround the world or that the best idea jumped out in the most absurd way and triggered a collection. They had dollars to spare and lacked the creative sensibility to know how to use the wonderful fabrics that Moretti presented them with. The economic aspect would always prevail over the artistic one.

By the time dessert was served, Aline had already envisaged possible future run-ins with them. She watched them, both chubby, with their air of superiority, trying to see what they couldn't. Well, that's where she came in…Without the money that Sassari had offered and which remained where he'd left it, everything could go belly up. She needed the job. When the Americans politely said goodbye on the terrace before a coffee, she digested the outcome.

"I know what you're thinking. They're not Renzo, and leaving Europe is difficult, but you need to," said Guido.

He was thinking about his widowhood and Aline about the consequences of her marriage; she'd relived it with Ahmed in a devastating way. Guido's gaze, insightful and deep, alerted her despite the fact that she'd never shown him her cards.

"You must learn to break with the past. I am an expert at that. I know you want to get away from here." His firm and determined voice confirmed the urgency that pushed her to flee, not knowing exactly where to. "You'll adapt to the newness." And for a moment doubted the wisdom of confiding his thoughts to her but did so all the same. "I made a trip with your father to Israel…"

Baffled, Aline realized how wrong she'd been in thinking that Patricia was the last surprise. There was another in store that time had hidden in order to reveal it at the right moment.

"It was shortly before Henry died. He asked that I accompany him, aware of the extent of his illness. We visited the places he longed to see, and we stayed at my wife's house in Beit Hakerem, where my son now lives." Guido carried on while he showed her some photos.

The images showed Aline's father with his unmistakable nostalgic air that did not imply despondency, strolling through the old Jerusalem neighborhoods or sitting at a bar terrace on the waterfront of Tel Aviv. Others, taken by a third party, bore witness to his tour of the Degania kibbutz and, in the last ones, on the back of a camel in the Negev desert.

"Why didn't you tell me about that trip?" Aline replied, deeply moved, unable to prevent a profound feeling of helplessness from taking hold.

"It was not the right time; now it is. Go, and as we say in Hebrew, you'll see which way the wind blows. Disconnect, follow in his footsteps, and live that experience. I'm convinced that upon your return, you'll have the answers."

"Was he also looking for answers?" she asked without taking her eyes off the old photos. "I thought he had them all."

"Henry was always clear-headed about things. It was the circumstances that made him lead an unexpected existence. He owed that journey to his innermost conscience."

And Aline parsed the dialectical battles between her father and grandfather, which now took on a special relevance after this revelation. Guido ordered more coffee and moved on.

"My son Michael is thirty-three years old. As a good Jew, he's confident in what he does. He is a journalist living his dream in what he considers idyllic conditions. He often says that he lives on the confines of the end. Perhaps I'll have to assume my old age alone. When his mother died, we returned to Italy, confident that when the time came, he'd join the family business. I was mistaken. Go and stay at his place. He's very independent and leads a frantic life. What do you think? In just over a month, you must sign a contract and move to New York."

Aline ran her eyes over the yellowed portraits.

"I will go to Israel. This is certain. Can you help me organize it?"

Guido knew that he owed it to Henry, who, on so many occasions, had helped him overcome his past.

Ahmed was still on the deck of the Sapphire, unable to erase from his memory the look of fear on Aline's face when he asked her about Bürke. During the conversation, he guessed that something had overwhelmed her. Something more serious, unrelated to the proposal that Bürke, in his name, had made to her that night.

Rachid Massoud, his sagacious right-hand man, was the perfect person to discover what had happened. He had done so with the news regarding Partana's death and of Aline being his wife. At the time, Rahhal thought that he'd lost a good contact for his business dealings but was free to try and win over his widow. Now, after that conversation with Aline, he was absolutely sure that their lives had crossed because it was meant.

Massoud moved with ease in troubled waters and was a good negotiator when it came to dealing with the upper echelons of the Lebanese government. His patience was infinite, and he had nerves of steel. He did not react like the other Arabs, who followed their emotions, but instead analyzed each step thoroughly before making decisions, not like Ahmed, who put them off till the last minute because he believed more in intuition than deliberation.

Ahmed felt that to win over Aline, the first thing was to rescue her from her past, and Bürke, for some reason, was part of it. He would give anything for her, even if she was Jewish and he Arab. He would change his plans and return to Beirut and summon Massoud at the summer house in Bhamdoum. A few days of rest would do him good, and trekking in the nearby mountains would bring him peace. It's what he wanted, apart from Aline.

CHAPTER 9

ROME, 1974

Haim was waiting for his agents in the austere safe house on Via Barberini. He had to remain neutral given the difficult situation that Aline, ignorant of the facts, had created for him the previous night. She wanted to say goodbye before her departure. They met at a family restaurant in Trastevere. During dinner, he perceived that the unbreakable friendship that united them, despite the hidden truths, remained intact. He watched her keenly as she filled him in, at times hesitantly, with a certain indefinite air between boldness and caution, regarding her conversation with Guido.

Before the old photos on a checkered tablecloth, Haim answered her questions subtly so that she wouldn't suspect that his knowledge of Israel came from his occasional visits. He filled her in on the places Henry had visited, like a competent tour guide, all while the images of walking through Jerusalem with Hanna and how much he had mourned her flooded his mind. Since he was aware of the activities of the Santacroce, he encouraged her, later regretting having listened to her.

The flimsy stability that sustained his friend's daily fluctuations was about to crack. He realized it right away as she lowered her voice and unfolded a note written in Arabic, and asked if he could help her decipher it. Aline knew that he'd take Arabic classes while living in Paris. Haim immediately realized that he was dealing with an arms delivery in Syria since the dates and locations were stipulated between the lines, and the Norseman's nickname danced between signs. The surname Partana was written in a corner, but it was clear to him that he was merely a link between Bürke and the Arabs.

With the intention of downplaying the evidence and thinking over the appropriate answer so that she would accept it at face value, he asked, "What should we order for dessert? Tiramisu or cassata? By the way, where did you get it from?"

He was sure that she wouldn't lie to him, for her answer had to be consistent with the text of the documents that she'd just handed him. Aline, aware of this fact, made an effort to remain calm when she confessed that she'd stolen it from the yacht of some acquaintances in Nice. He seemed convinced while he, on the other hand, lied to her by the candlelight that lit their faces.

"It appears that they were making a transaction to acquire a boat. Did your husband like to sail? It seems that they shared hobbies."

There was no other choice. From the moment he sounded the alarm and the chain of command gave the green light to intervene, Aline would clearly be at risk.

Aline shrugged her shoulders, totally unaware that she'd just given the Mossad a most valuable piece of information, let alone that Bürke's nickname had cropped up on those papers. She finished her tiramisu and, without hesitation, said, "I think it's best to get rid of this." And with a determined gesture, she burned what she thought had been Marco's last passion, a new yacht.

Haim returned to his flat and his thoughts. The conversations with his confidants in the evening, when it was time to report in detail on the tactics to follow and plan the next steps, ended up rattling their nerves on more than one occasion. They'd smoke one cigarette after another, and as time passed, the atmosphere became unbreathable. His men had been tracking Bürke since Haim's meeting with the SID colonel, but his whereabouts were still unknown. There was no evidence either that he'd left the country, at least with the passport registered under the SID.

Haim poured himself a strong coffee and set out to write the encrypted message that he'd deliver to his contact at the embassy. He would send the message by radio to the corresponding department, where an analyst, along with his superior, a former army general, would verify the information before proceeding. It was clear that Yurchenko's arms, controlled by Bürke, would end up in the hands of terrorists who, undoubtedly, would use them to attack Israel.

His memory easily retained dates and places of delivery: June 30, twenty kilometers south of Palmira, and six days later, the second delivery, thirteen kilometers west of Al-Sukhnah. Eighteen days till the first delivery was to be made. As soon as the headquarters in Tel Aviv notified him of the go-ahead for the operation and dispatched the security forces, he would give the latter a background on Aline's identity. From that moment onwards, he'd ask for counter-surveillance measures for what might occur. His boss was fond of saying, "If you're not part of the solution, you must be part of the problem." She wavered between these two possibilities. Haim had always told her that fate was in one's hands, but it clearly was playing hard to get.

At that moment, her friend was on her way to Tel Aviv. Bürke was missing, and the Mossad would act if necessary.

He needed to go down to the street and clear his head. He had always wanted to protect Aline ever since meeting her, but he could swear that some dark forces were conspiring against it.

ISRAEL

Romema was a neighborhood full of offices and industrial buildings. Michael parked on Yirmiyahu Street in front of the long, two-story building that housed the offices of *The Jerusalem Post*. The second floor had a number of windows, behind which the reporters worked tirelessly.

Endless meetings awaited him. He kept a chaotic agenda ever since he was tasked with supervising international affairs on top of specializing in domestic politics. Milan was a distant memory, as was the year in which, after completing his degree, he began working at *Corriere della Sera*, starting from the bottom. His insight and tenacity were his best allies in that "jungle," as he used to call the newsroom. Back then, whenever he had some vacation time, he'd spend it at the house inherited from his mother in Beit Hakerem and perfecting his Hebrew till he managed to speak it without an accent.

As soon as the opportunity to join *The Jerusalem Post* presented itself, he switched countries and newspapers, certain that his choice would give him a unique perspective and knowledge. Despite his seniority, when he started out at *The Post,* he went through several sections until he got where he aspired to be. His slogan was "you will start the day without knowing how you are going to end it," and, of course, at times found himself in real danger. Each risky report and the Yom Kippur War strengthened his character, already energetic in itself, and set him further apart from his father, who was not too happy that he lived amid this insecurity. The latter's call to inform him that the daughter of his friend Henry would be staying in his place for two or three weeks put him in an awkward position which he wasn't too happy about.

He got out of the car and felt the mid-June heat. He entered the crowded room and went over to his table, where he set out to analyze the information before heading off to Parliament for a long debate. On his return, he had to write his column in a great hurry, as well as to write several pages of the unfinished book that his publisher kept pressuring him about. This meant many sleepless nights. All he needed was to take care of Aline Asher.

Aline landed late in the afternoon at Ben Gurion airport, hectic and chaotic. The passengers on her flight, like herself, patiently resigned themselves to the interrogation at the security controls. When it was her turn, she tried to be concise regarding her reasons for visiting the country. If she had elaborated, the questions might have dragged on for hours.

While she waited for her bags, she grasped the people's rhythm, frenzied and noisy, as well as the patent cold and contained tension that could be felt in the air. She got into a taxi, and the perception that she was moving away from her problems made her cognizant of her lack of balance. The airport was left behind, and as the car climbed toward Jerusalem, she reached the conclusion that there was still a lot that she needed to learn before she could become serene. Impetuous and irresponsible in her actions, she had lied to the Lamberts and to Haim. She sought refuge in Patricia, who, without deserving it, gave her unconditional help. She was barely able to articulate a few words when they said goodbye at Villa Balbini.

She had ceased to express her deep feelings since her marriage collapsed like a house of cards, and this forced her to lie. She had trouble discerning where the truth ended and the quicksand began; that cut and thrust is what she'd now face with Michael, for journalists have a tendency to ask more questions than the rest of mortals, and nothing escaped their judgment.

She entered the neighborhood of Beit Hakerem, which brimmed with an English spirit, and felt her nostalgia slowly disappearing on realizing that she was in a place that might offer her some respite. The taxi stopped in front of a house on Schiller Street, one of many that had two stories and were surrounded by pines and cedars. She was surprised to see that, despite the years that had elapsed, they were identical to those in the photos that she kept in her suitcase. The roofs still had the original red bricks, and the silent exposed stone walls, perhaps witnesses of innumerable experiences, seemed to confirm it. She grabbed her light luggage and followed Guido's directions. The neighbor had

Michael's keys, since his return home was always unpredictable.

Yael Bel, red-haired and talkative, greeted her as if she were a distant relative she was waiting for. Wearing her apron and with an attitude of one who is accustomed to performing such duties, she accompanied her through the garden to her new abode. Full of naturalness, she showed her the ground floor, which consisted of two large rooms joined together. The tall rectangular windows, which began practically at floor level and allowed for plenty of light, stood out. From the simple living room, equipped with functional furniture and maroon-colored upholstered sofas, one passed into a room whose walls lined with bookcases hoarded an infinity of books. In the center, in front of the window, a table and a typewriter surrounded by papers suggested that Michael had spent hours there. The kitchen, impersonal but practical, breathed the disorder of the man who moves about alone. Yael opened the fridge.

"Just in case…" she remarked in passable English. "Sometimes there is nothing."

But a platter of stuffed eggplants and a note that read in Italian, "heat in the oven if I'm late," sat in the fridge. Aline figured that the wooden table surrounded by chairs was the only dining table in the house since the original had been converted into an office.

They climbed the stairs, leaving the rest of the rooms behind them. Yael left Aline in hers at the end of the corridor, gave her the keys, and advised her to organize herself. Guido's son had no set schedule.

If she'd been told months earlier that she would find herself retracing her father's footsteps in a house in

Jerusalem whose owner she did not know, she would've never believed it. She opened the balcony door; the first star appeared in the sky.

The distant tapping of the typewriter woke her up. She looked at her watch. It was one in the morning. She'd fallen asleep on top of the patchwork quilt that covered the bed with her clothes on. The room, like the rest of the house, exuded comfort, even with its minimal decoration. Drowsy, she wandered to the bathroom and doused her face with cold water before tiptoeing downstairs. She halted momentarily, leaning against the study's doorjamb, and examined its surroundings. He immediately noticed her presence.

Michael, dark-skinned and auburn hair, strong without being robust, seemed to have a seamless complicity with himself. Impossible to conceive of a man more different from his father in his physical appearance and, as she assumed, in his way of being. Guido, without forgetting his roots but trying to enjoy every moment to the fullest, was the opposite of an idealistic son who exposed himself in a country that was not exempt from risks and with certain discomforts. As he stepped up to greet her, she noticed that his features betrayed weariness.

"I was unable to call, but I knew Yael would take care of you." He spoke to her in Italian, with a slightly imprecise accent.

A warm wind blew in through the half-open windows, and Aline recognized in him a man dedicated to his profession and with a well-defined character. After thanking him for his hospitality and seeing the half-written page sticking out of the Olivetti, she realized that he needed to continue with his work, so she told him about her plans.

"I'm an unexpected visitor, and I don't want to disturb you." She stressed the fact that her presence would not disrupt his daily routine.

Michael, exhausted, was in no mood to carry on a conversation, but when she told him that she was planning to visit the old quarter in the morning, he offered to accompany her in his car to the Jaffa Gate, trusting that she knew how to navigate the bowels of Jerusalem without being foolhardy.

He took a map from a shelf and spread it out under the desk light; he showed her the area's entrances and warned her to take certain precautions. He told her that if she wanted to go with him, he'd wake her up early. She agreed and left him in the dim light of the room so that he could continue with his work, which, judging by the number of sheets of paper everywhere, must've completely absorbed him. She tried to remember if she'd ever seen Marco amid books or papers but was unable.

Michael, before carrying on with the difficulties of the blank page before him, realized that due to the informational effort caused by the presidential elections, he had neglected to ask his father about the reason why Aline had traveled to Israel. His critical eye told him there was a compelling reason for Henry Asher's daughter to be sleeping on the floor above. He would try to find out.

In the kitchen, flooded with light and more relaxed than in the middle of the night, they spent just enough time breakfasting. Michael shot a glance at the woman who, the previous night, due to the fatigue and the study's gloom, he'd been unable to properly observe. He thought her attractive and of a vague nationality. He wouldn't have known how to classify her. He listened to his own opinion, which advised him to be cautious, but the strange thing was that, for some reason, he wanted to know more. He blamed it on the implicit curiosity of his profession and his own. He asked her if she had slept well and if she was comfortable in her room. He didn't believe to be off the mark in thinking that she could find her way around anywhere in the world.

When there was not a drop of coffee left in the cups, he fixed his dark, nervous eyes on Aline's and asked her the question that revealed Guido's discretion.

"I wonder where our parents' friendship stems from. I'd like to know."

"From far back," she answered, not at all sure of the convenience of uncovering the how and where of their meeting and the explanations that this would entail.

"Golda Meir used to say that confidences are dissected in the kitchen, but you'd better tell me about it tonight at a restaurant that's a must in this city," Michael replied as he grabbed his car keys, betraying his haste.

An accepted silence came between the two, and each drew their own conclusions. Michael, always on the hunt for the finest story, sensed that he had one nearby; and Aline, in turn, that it was best to be cautious. Sassari was explicit enough about it.

They climbed into the Volkswagen, and he instructed her on each of the emblematic constructions that they came across. They were at the Jaffa Gate in less than half an hour. The square was full of life. Michael hesitated before leaving her in the midst of the bustling crowd. Knowing that he was her only contact in the country, gave her his direct extension at *The Post* and suggested that she take a taxi home before dark. The "beetle" was immediately engulfed by the chaotic traffic, and she by the old city.

The contrast of old and new and people of different races created a mixture of sensations that Aline had never felt before, as if each stone had a meaning and could be evoked in a different way.

She ventured into the Armenian neighborhood, map in hand, and with an established route traced the previous evening. As she moved toward the Wailing Wall, she realized that that was where heavenly matters were dealt with. The soul, the big questions, and the reasons for one's existence were alive and present. That's why her father traveled all the way here. She descended steps in-between antique shops, essences, and scents. An endless number of languages accompanied her. She didn't want to linger in the narrow streets or travel through their history; she'd have plenty of time for that. She wanted to reach the Wall as soon as possible.

She could still hear Guido's words telling her, "That place belongs to you and you to it; it was Henry's first stop."

She continued to make her way straight down David Street and the Arab Quarter bazaars till she reached Chain Street. She turned right and walked down a small alley that ended at a solemn staircase. At the end of it were the Esplanade and the Wall, whose stone blocks, of a worn-out color and of considerable height, were most imposing. The enclosure gave off a special energy. A great peace filled the atmosphere, despite the uniformed soldiers' watchful eyes and a constant flow of people. She passed a police checkpoint and walked toward the part of the Wall destined for women's prayers.

This was the first time she tried talking to God without blaming Him for her misfortunes. She told Him that she was willing to accept her father's death and have faith in the future despite years of distress. She heard the soft murmur of prayers around her but chose instead to detach herself from religious beliefs and think of a single superior being, as Haim said, ever-present. She turned her gaze on the men engrossed in their prayers and imagined her father entrusting his life and those he abandoned. She rested her hands on the Wall and felt the morning dew on the stones. She took out a small notebook that she carried in her bag and wrote her wish, folded the paper, and placed it in one of the fissures.

The day had dawned cloudy, but the sun was beginning to make its appearance. She lifted her head. A rainbow covered the Esplanade and the Dome of the Rock, disappearing into the horizon. Those colored arches were sent by God from heaven to make His presence felt. That's what her father told her once when she, in her youth, saw them appear at the edge of the forest at the farmhouse. With the certainty and serenity that he had heard her, she retraced her steps.

Three thousand kilometers from Jerusalem, on the western coast of the Odessa Bay, on the shores of the Black Sea, the Greek freighter Helios, flying a Liberian flag, was anchored. The Yugoslav captain, Borgan Sulok, a hard-drinking man, finished off his first whiskey while placing his cap on his reddish hair. He narrowed his gray eyes to make sure that the Soviet trucks on land were ready for the ship's crane boom to lift aboard the heavy wooden boxes that they were transporting. Packed with German MP40 and MP41 submachine guns and Yugoslav bazookas, they could arm more than six hundred men.

Looking relaxed, Sulok went to hand over the last user certificate, forged, of course, which had been sent to him by one of Yurchenko's men. He had earned the latter's trust, given his impeccable command of the sea, languages, and the manner in which he went about solving critical situations.

Wasyl Yurchenko bought the weapons in the Soviet Union, paid in advance, and, in this particular case, the necessary paperwork to transport them had been issued by a commercial manager of the Sudanese Embassy in Greece who, like him, got paid and kept quiet. Everything was in order, except that they would not be docking in Sudan but in the port of Latakia in Syria, although no one would control this.

At last, the five thousand tons of the Helios put to sea and plowed those dark waters under a blazing sun in the middle of June. Three days later, it would cross the Bosphorus and refuel in Istanbul. It would take nine long days of sailing through the Greek islands to Latakia.

The captain blurted out his favorite phrase to the crew, "Let's hurry up slowly," with some reason, for they had to time their arrival with the Syrian inspector's turn at the dock. He was the one who had to come on board to collect the cargo's bill of landing. Documents that

Yurchenko's man had entrusted him with that specified that they were transporting spare parts for automobiles.

That June day, as was planned, the Syrian authorized the unloading and, once the cargo was on land, checked that the number of boxes corresponded to those on the bill of lading before the merchandise was dispatched into some old Renault trucks. Without losing sight of them, Sulok, who enjoyed a certain camaraderie with the Syrian, invited him to have coffee in the port's dilapidated coffee shop. Sitting on the wooden chairs, the inspector chatted about his things, arching his eyebrows to the beat of his words. The captain listened while he watched carefully as the boxes were being placed on the vehicles. If something went wrong or one of them were to break, the order was to bribe whomever it took; and the Syrian was bribable. Sulok made sure to prolong the conversation till the trucks took off and disappeared in an unknown direction.

Michael called her at home to let her know that he was running late and that he'd go straight from work to The American Colony Hotel's terrace, that she should wait for him there.

At the same time that Sulok was finishing his third coffee, Aline entered the building, the former palace of a pasha, where diplomats, royalty, and journalists met.

As night fell, and surrounded by trees, birds, and palm trees, Aline ordered a fruit juice while waiting for this man who conveyed the feeling of doing things with such an intensity that it appeared as if each one was the last act of his life. Michael showed up looking weary but lucid and quick in his conversation. He asked the waiter for a glass of wine that took several few minutes to arrive, long enough for him to take an interest in her day. Aline told him, leaving out her feelings at the Wall and adding her hasty lunch of hummus and falafel in the old quarter before visiting the Tower of David Museum. With the chirping birds around them, Michael raised his glass.

"Let's make a toast. Here we usually do it for life."

Aline did so, hoping to avoid picking up the conversation that was left hanging in the kitchen, and asked him about his work.

"Sheikh Abu Talal Alzama debated in Parliament today, and I couldn't miss it. He's a Bedouin, Member of Parliament, and a friend of mine. He never disappoints. He will assert his rights just as he will put his ear to the sand to know if someone is approaching his camp," he replied without taking his eyes off her.

"Your world and mine are quite different," Aline remarked, keeping in mind the sophistication of Renzo's atelier and a cosmopolitan Guido choosing patterns in Como.

She elaborated, describing what she did for a living and the contract she was hoping to sign, which would keep her away from Europe.

"Neither your collections nor my columns are transcendental, but rather what you believe in. If we agreed on this, our worlds would be closer," he said.

Marco sneaked into Aline's mind for a split second. Had she reasoned like him, she wouldn't be in Jerusalem at this moment. Her mistake was assuming, upon meeting him, that she had fallen in love with him – a stranger at the time.

"What are you thinking?" Michael asked, intending to delve deeper into the woman whom he still couldn't figure out why she was sleeping at his place.

Concealing her thoughts, Aline replied that she'd like to hear about his experiences in Israel and learn more about his profession, which he took to, in her opinion, like a duck to water.

"I have this bad habit of looking for answers," he said. "Sometimes, we journalists tend to come face to face with uncomfortable truths. Publishing them is risky, but I will tell you one or two."

Not for a moment did she doubt that Guido's son was an expert in uncovering these truths in the shortest time possible.

During dinner, he was most pleasant, answering her questions till she relaxed to such an extent that her worries seemed practically imperceptible. Before dessert, a typical honey tart, she looked at him with her slanted eyes—which Partana described as knives—and, with confidence, confessed something that she wouldn't have the previous night, "Our parents met about twelve years ago in Patricia di Borgo's villa in Como. She was my father's mistress and a friend of yours. That is where I met Guido. We hit it off and became good friends."

"I hadn't the slightest idea. We're so different that we avoid talking about our surroundings. We'd argue."

Sensing that he was eager to hear about this episode, she carried on, "You see, our parents had a few things in common, their roots and having to flee because of the war; Patricia, naturally, and a trip they made together to Israel when mine didn't have much time left. The idea of my coming was your father's. He's convinced that I will return knowing which is the best path for me to follow."

"What is hindering it?"

"My mistakes."

"As long as you're alive, you can correct them," Michael stated with conviction, though she wondered whether her marriage to the Foreigner would ever stop conditioning her. "Are you married?"

"I separated. We were different. Our principles were as far apart as the Earth is from Pluto."

"Time puts things in their rightful place, you'll see. Now we have to organize that Henry's memories and this country join forces so as to unearth your priority."

"And which is yours?" Aline enquired.

"Mine was assimilating what it means to be a Jew and changing course to get to know Israel and its people. My profession allowed me to do this."

"And now you know?"

"I know that what once was must be remembered, but the future is waiting for us. The truth is simple, but we tend to approach it the hard way."

Aline felt those words touch her heart.

He tried to find out more and asked about Henry, but Aline shut down, saying she didn't wish to talk about him at the moment.

As night fell, Michael began to consider that Aline was like a book that grabs you, and you're eager to know the ending.

The following weeks were organized by Michael, in which they pursued the routes and places that she wanted to discover. Aline took pleasure in her visits to museums that were interspersed with days in which she, along with Yael, toured the country in the latter's Jeep. They visited the Degania Alef kibbutz and discovered on the Tel Aviv waterfront that the bar where Guido and Henry drank beers was still standing. They walked along the beach, on whose shores Aline sheltered with her memories. She seemed to have shed the cobweb that had wrapped her up and to once again be the girl that she was before the damned rowboat went adrift. Nothing wobbled.

Michael, absorbed by his work, tried to find time to spend with her, which never crossed his mind that he'd do when his father first called. Between one meeting and the next, he took her to visit the inside of Parliament and to have a snack in its dining room, jam-packed with somber faces with signs of concern. Dinners in the typical restaurants that only the locals knew about became commonplace; but the days went by quickly, the nights too, and he began to realize the difficulty of being intimate with Henry's daughter, who, in his opinion, held more secrets than the government and the Mossad combined. That was his impression after fine-tuning his senses, just like when he followed a unique scoop. Although little by little, he realized that he was not only moved by a professional interest; there were other feelings hitherto ignored by him.

This evening had to be like all others, in which Aline chose her reading from his bookshelf and hung out reading in the living room while he wrote the articles that, no matter what, he had to hand in the following morning. But it didn't happen that way.

Michael watched her from the corner of his eye as she touched the books with her fingers as if caressing them. Suddenly, a book caught her eye, and as if she had discovered a treasure, she looked up, grabbed it, and held it out to him, showing him the inscription on one of its pages. It read thus: "To Guido, for our days in Beit Hakerem. Henry."

"Do you want to talk about him?" Michael suggested. He had long sensed the importance of Henry in Aline's life.

"We better talk about Guido. He called today. He said he needed to have our news."

Aline felt that it was the right moment to present to him what had been on her mind for a long time. Her words had to be firm and straightforward. She risked coming clean despite Michael's eerie silence, which reminded her of those between Henry and Samuel during their conversations in the stone house.

"Forget the differences with your father. Be above them and meet with him. I'm sure this is possible now that I know you both. 'To believe in the same thing, that's what counts.' You told me so the night after I arrived, while we were dining on the terrace of The Colony Hotel. Do you remember?" She didn't wait for an answer and continued, "You two believe in the same thing. That's what should unite you. How you each live your life is just a simple choice. Henry got Guido to put the present before the past; now his future is you."

Michael processed his life in a few seconds. If he was in Jerusalem, it was because his father had made the right decision: He fled to America, saving him from a more than uncertain fate. This reasoning was what made him propose to Aline that they sit under the porch at the back of the house and for her to talk to him about that great stranger to him: Guido.

Accompanied only by a soft night breeze, Aline narrated all that she knew about him.

It was almost dawn when Michael had already imbued himself with more than explicit descriptions of his father and his surroundings. He was struck by how she had captured Guido's personality and true character, hidden beneath that cloak that his work provided him with and that now came across as not so superficial. That solid friendship with Henry—of whom, this time around, she also spoke about in-depth—as well as of Pat's story that united the three of them, penetrated so deep within him that at the end of the confidences, he told Aline that he needed a few hours sleep before going to *The Post*.

She breathed easy as they entered the house from the garden. She had achieved her purpose without having to mention the real reason that took her to Como, but she couldn't help but think about Pat and how she'd be worried for her, about the steps she still had to take, and about the life that awaited her in New York.

Before they each retired to their room, Aline heard a "thank you" that she hadn't expected. Michael had understood the great union that existed between Aline and

Henry, and although the latter was no longer around, he became a key element that allowed him to see from another prism the life of his own father and their relationship.

BEIRUT

Bürke was staying at the Phoenicia Hotel. The tension from the continuous trips and the succession of airports, hotels, and previous negotiations before closing the deals for Yurchenko's clients had left him exhausted.

He came out of his room and made his way to the eleventh floor. The restaurant Eau de Vie awaited him, modern and glamorous, with priceless views of the Mediterranean that made him curse for not being on his boat. His bodyguards sat on the bar stools, and he waited for Georges Haleemi, Rahhal's cousin, to arrive with his men while he savored an arak at a table in the large bar. Eau de Vie was one of his favorite joints when in the city for business, although that afternoon's affair was no small matter.

The trucks that left Latakia for the south of Palmyra, loaded to the brim with weapons, were intercepted by mercenaries—or so they thought—who, besides murdering his and George's drivers, had seized the weapons. Knowing the bowels of the business, he concluded that the work had been carried out by professionals. The region was a powder keg in which there were infinite possibilities, from mercenaries acting on their own or paid by a third party to Kurdish terrorists. His bewilderment was matched by his irritation. He wasn't sure of anything, but being an old fox in these matters, he had to find the infiltrated mole who had betrayed them, in addition to replacing the Lebanese's weapons, or he would lose the client and his life.

In all the years that those regular and precise shipments had been operating, never had there been an attack of this nature. Wasyl's reputation and his own were in jeopardy, as was the business itself. He would divert the second freighter, the Khysos, packed with the arms that Georges was now expecting and which was sailing along the same route as the Helios had only a few days earlier. On his orders, the Khysos would dock at the port of Tartus, and his men would drive the trucks to Jordan to make the delivery outside the small town of Shajara.

Those were the thoughts running through his head when Georges appeared, with his elegant blue blazer, his hair slicked back, and those manners which he'd picked up in the best English schools and which bestowed upon him a look of impeccability. His bodyguards stood in the back, at the bar, watching over his safety.

Bürke got on well with him, perhaps because he was more liberal and European than his cousin Ahmed, whose origins marked his behavior. He did business with the former and provided the latter with women and contacts. The Lebanese ordered a coffee and expressed his dissatisfaction. He'd been doing business with Wasyl for years, whom he considered efficient and feared by his people, and suddenly he discovered a vulnerability in him that had affected his commitments. Erik's head was spinning as he listened, just like the ice cubes in the glass of arak he was nursing when he assured him of the arms replacement and shared his suspicions with him.

"As regards your first point, I don't have the slightest doubt in my mind. As for your conclusions," Georges pulled a face that could've expressed either astonishment or understanding while he processed the information, "if they keep foiling your shipments, you and Wasyl will be ruined. I hope there are no more setbacks in the shipment that is on its way."

"I've changed the route," Bürke specified. "For security's sake."

His muscles tightened. Georges' attitude when they closed the deal about that arms shipment in Nice aboard the Sapphire came to mind. He seemed restless that day. One had the feeling that a parallel matter had completely monopolized his attention. The acquired experience was warning him that something unexpected had truncated his mathematical plans. Georges had collaborators who could betray him, but he probably didn't even consider this.

Erik, without preamble, made clear his surprise at his behavior the day they carried out the now defunct operation.

"You're not in the habit of taking notes. But you did that day. You were about to lose your temper…And I had nothing to do with that."

That line of thinking put Georges on the alert and in an even lousier mood. He wondered if he should mention what had happened because it'd be worse than the Norseman making false assumptions; he might start pulling at a string in that big blunder of his, over which he lost control. He stopped turning it over in his mind.

"I lost the Sapphire to a poker of aces the night before we met. I was confident that the *Baraka* would be on my side. I was wrong. *Voilá.*" He elaborated without telling him about his desperation and the sleepless night spent up to his ears in booze. "When we met, my head was exploding. That is the reason for the notes."

Bürke was aware that gambling, more than any other vice, was his client's downfall, but when he informed him of the loss, he understood his agitation before such a blunder. He began to fear the worst. He would've grabbed him and shaken the hell out of him. He tried to hold the bad omens in check. Of all the nights that Georges went to any of the casinos scattered around the world, it had to be the day before their meeting when he lost the Sapphire…A damn twist of fate. Given the trust that existed between them, he asked him where those jottings had ended up after ordering a double whiskey to cushion the next discovery.

"You dashed off to the airport, and I was in a hurry to get back to the casino and convince my opponent to accept cash instead of taking the Sapphire. I left the briefcase open, overflowing with documents, in the deck lounge after our conversation. I was so busy finalizing details of that ill-fated incident that I didn't notice the disappearance of that piece of paper. Especially since my memory hadn't failed me, and I'd registered all the information that you'd given me."

Bürke, expectant, leaned his body on the table and, with the same aim as the best hunter before his coveted prey, spoke, "I am going to ask you a crucial question. Did anyone outside of your people come aboard that day?"

Georges reflected. The crew had been with him for years, and his bodyguards would've alerted him of any intrusion; then, as the conversation progressed, he relived the image of the girl leaving the boat when he arrived. He was beside himself before his opponent's refusal, who turned down the deal that he'd offered him.

"No stranger did, except for a woman I passed in the evening when I got back on board. She'd spent some time with Ahmed in the same room where I'd left my documents. I found that out later."

"Do you know her name and why she was there?"

"Her name is Aline. He met her in Ibiza," he replied, a trace of doubt settling in his brain.

Erik's blood ran cold. It could only be Aline Partana. She'd lived with Marco for years, and he figured that she was aware of his shenanigans. Perhaps she'd become a professional in the service of some organization interested in the movements of the Lebanese. Given Ahmed's fascination with her, it was easy for her to have used him for her own ends or for whomever she worked for. Too many facts had come together since the night Rahhal had offered her the fabulous diamond.

"I'll look into it," Erik stated in his gruff voice, without revealing his dealings with Partana's wife ever since he caught a glimpse of her naked in his pool.

Then, using as an excuse the fact Ahmed was not involved in arms trafficking, he suggested that it would be best not to alert him until he had evidence of Aline's movements. He wasn't at ease till Georges was in agreement and said so, all while he kept an eye on the spectacular girl crossing the bar.

"I have the same interest as you in getting to the bottom of this matter. I've lost credibility due to this mess.

Sometimes subtle women finish off the jobs better than any mercenary," Georges stated.

Bürke drained his whiskey. He figured that if she was capable of marrying Partana, she knew what she was getting into, but nobody was going to fuck him over. Neither would he fill Yurchenko in on his inquiries until he caught her and she confessed. He didn't know how far Aline's tentacles reached. He would contact Rome's chief inspector at the ministry of finance, who, like Sulok, drew a bonus and provided them with off-the-record information. In this case, he'd have to figure out how to reach the appropriate department to get the information. Aline was Partana's wife, who was listed as a person of interest. Nobody better than this inspector to find out if she had entered or left Italy, as well as her whereabouts. It would take him forty-eight hours to find out. He experienced a feeling of anticipated triumph.

NEGEV

Michael, with Henry's daughter at his side, drove the powerful Jeep on his way to Beersheva. The experience of sleeping in a Bedouin camp and spending a night in the desert was imperative for Aline, as it was for Michael, who wanted to tear down the barriers she erected between them.

The infinite desert threatened the existence at the very root of humankind. Michael was used to fighting and to deliberate, but for Aline, this impact would mean a reckoning with herself.

They crossed the steppe valley of Canaan between Beersheba and Arad and turned south into the Negev, with its dunes and sunbaked sand contrasting with the rocky, unyielding mountains, sometimes battered by the khamsin wind from the south-east. Silent, she discovered the breadth of the overwhelming landscape. There was no need for words. She now understood why Ahmed mentioned the desert and why her father wanted to see it and where Michael gave the impression of moving around with the same ease as he did in the streets of Jerusalem. With his skill, they reached the camp across sandy roads before the merciless sun beat down on it.

White tents, sewn by the skillful hands of women who had taken the direction of the wind into account, appeared in the near distance, as did camels, sheep, and goats. A young Bedouin, his skin burned and tanned by the sun, greeted them. He wore a white djellaba and over it a long jacket of the same color. The speckled *keffiyeh* that he wore on his head, in red, green, and blue colors, was fastened with double black cords.

"This is Aref, the son of Abu Talal, the sheikh," Michael explained. "The Arabs put 'Abu' in front of the names of men who are fathers as a sign of respect," he told her and informed her that no one spoke Hebrew.

What he didn't tell her is that Aref provided him with discreet and precise information and could tell before anyone else the tracks of terrorists and traffickers when they crossed the desert. In exchange, when Sheikh Talal Alzama needed that his demands get proper media repercussion, Michael made sure they did. The journalist knew the courage and wisdom of these wild and intrepid Bedouins, of primitive customs but loyal to their tribe. There was mutual respect.

The hospitality was immediate, and while Aref prepared sweet tea for them, as a sign that he wished them a pleasant life, and offered them cheese and bread, Michael explained the customs of those proud nomads, who prepared for life as if they were to live forever and for death as if they were to die the following day. He also told her about certain dangers involved in desert crossings and the sanctuary that travelers found in these communities. Aline was relieved to learn that if she tasted salt in her food, a bond was created that required the host to protect them for three days.

The dry heat increased as the day wore on. They approached the camels, who, with their padded feet and sad eyes above enormous nostrils, rested on those sands.

"Without them, the desert wouldn't be a desert," Michael assured her, "but we can't ride them today. The temperature will rise significantly."

He suggested an obligatory trek a little over an hour from the camp. This time he took the map out of his backpack. They'd cross the Negev till they reached the ruins of Ein Avdat. The rivers and waterfalls of the national park in a steep ravine where goats and gazelles roamed freely were a spectacle that left no one indifferent. And neither did the route nor Michael leave Aline indifferent.

Michael's genuineness, his toughness and character, conquered her with the passing of days. Love, like luck, shows up when no one calls it. Letting go would be an option, but the dilemma nagged at her; their worlds couldn't be more different, although he envisaged them close.

When dusk fell, allowing for the sand and mountains to take on different hues, from reddish to purple, they returned to camp tired, knowing that they'd shared an unforgettable experience.

They cooled off in a large reservoir, the same the cattle used to quench their thirst. Aref and his people had slaughtered a lamb in their honor, and a lavish dinner awaited them. On a small fire, the coffee pot heated an aromatic infusion. They sat on colorful rugs and leaned on cushions surrounded by Bedouins. At the end of the feast, they listened to the sheikh's son narrate his unusual existence and the environment in which they found themselves. Michael translated. This is how Aline learned that when spring arrived, the desert bushes took on a deep purple color as if to make it known that nature's ultimate purpose was to live.

They'd spent days in Beit Hakerem sharing the same roof, but nothing was comparable to the feeling of being together in the middle of dunes and star-studded skies. Every other place paled in comparison. They went out and looked at the heavenly vault. The silence was so crushing that it seemed as if one could hear it. Michael put his arm across her shoulder, as Partana and her father had done. Partana's was an erotic embrace; that of her father, protecting; and Michael's, sure of what he did and wanted.

Overwhelmed by the immensity of the surroundings, they retrieved their pasts and mutually entrusted them to each other. He told her about his childhood in New York and his youth later in Italy. She, her summers in the Ampurdán, and her walks with her grandfather Samuel. She told him that despite the latter's efforts to get the whole family to forget their beliefs after their flight, she never let go of the values that her father instilled in her or the culture of her ancestors. These proved fundamental in decisive moments of her life. She also explained how her friendship with Haim Weiss contributed to this process during her Paris years at the Lamberts. She then tiptoed around her marriage, and Michael, unexpectedly, informed her that no woman had so far tempted him to make that commitment. He sensed that not even in the deepest intimacy would Aline talk about her former husband. Why, he'd also have to find out.

This perception prompted him to change argument, so after handing her a jacket—the temperature was dropping fast—he explained the continuing risks that he'd faced since leaving his comfortable position at the *Corriere della Sera.*

"For quite some time, I was in charge of covering events for the newspaper, at the front line, along with the army. There were times when I considered life and death in a matter of seconds and had no choice but to bet on risky decisions."

Aline knew very well what he meant, for she herself had lived through very similar circumstances during her life with Partana. And as if Michael wanted to warn her of what might happen, he went on, "Now that I am in permanent contact with politicians, I know how hard it is to negotiate without losing what you love. I deal with Arabs every day, and I can assure you that it's part of their culture to reach the truth after many conversations. We Israelis are more direct."

That remark brought to mind Aline's last line of reasoning aboard the Sapphire with Ahmed Rahhal. It seemed to her that he kept much more to himself than he let on. She hoped that she'd not see him again, despite his apologies and the Lebanese's conviction that they'd meet again.

Time had slipped by as quickly as the water in the springs at Ein Avdat. She would've much rather slept in his arms under the stars, but the customs of their hosts prevailed. She'd sleep with the other women and children. Michael approached the large tent with special interest and asked Aline, "That wonderful place that you always return to, what did you say it was called?"

"A *masía*."

"And what is a *masía*?"

"It is a rural farmhouse surrounded by a forest of pines and oaks. They're usually a few kilometers away from the Mediterranean coast. Mine is in the Ampurdán. I was happy there."

"You will be happy. You have dreams to fulfill, and dreams are like the Hebrew alphabet: It doesn't necessarily need to end with twenty-two letters."

Aline wanted to tell him that she regretted the years spent with Marco, that he'd left her a poisoned inheritance, but she was silent and whispered "good night" to him.

She tried in vain to sleep on the thin sheep's wool mattress, covering herself with a blanket that the Bedouins themselves had woven for days. Those endless hours of insomnia made her realize that she was an Asher and that she would not resign herself to the Santacroces conditioning her life. She'd create a collection for Americans equal to or better than the one she made for Renzo. The next day, Michael would tell her what he expected of her. She read it in his eyes.

Erik hung up the phone in his room at the Phoenicia Hotel in Beirut. The Roman inspector had just finished giving him the date and flight number on which Aline boarded for Tel Aviv. He got up from the sofa in a rage. The forebodings that gripped him forced him to make calculations. She had flown to Israel just a few days after spending the afternoon with Ahmed on the Sapphire. He suspected that she stole information to give to those who intercepted his trucks with the precision of someone who knows what he's doing. This woman drove him nuts. Each time his path crossed Aline's, his and Yurchenko's foundations wobbled. If she turned Ahmed down in Ibiza, it was because she was married to Partana. Now, widow, what was she doing in the Sapphire in Nice? She was not the type of person who was in a place without a purpose. He remembered Marco at his country house when he asked him for a special girl to forget her. This and the more than strange coincidences confirmed his suspicions that she was working for someone effective and more powerful than the Santacroces and that, perhaps, not even Marco found out who his wife really was.

He feared Yurchenko, who demanded that he root out whoever it was that betrayed them. He had only one option left: Locate her in Israel. His liaisons had certain contacts in the immigration department and would be able to find out in the entry log that listed the passengers' temporary addresses. The country's short distances favored his plan. She couldn't be too far from the spot where he intended to deliver the weapons in four days' time. It was a matter of coming up with a coldly calculated plan and executing it quickly.

It was dawning when they got ready to leave the camp. Michael was expected at *The Post* to prepare for his trip. Accredited along with other media, he would travel with the Minister of Foreign Affairs to Italy to cover the latter's engagements. The El Al flight would take off early in the morning the next day. His presence on this occasion was essential, not only because of his close relations with the country's press but also because of the Italian, English, and Hebrew, which he spoke flawlessly. This is what he was telling Aline as he placed the backpacks inside the Jeep, knowing that she's turned the essence of his life upside down the night before. This was not the time to tell her that he yearned for her and that she'd become someone special without her even trying. In her confession under the stars, he felt the depth of her thinking. He'd been captivated by her feelings, that way of hers of not avoiding commitments without renouncing the adventure.

Aref and the other men prayed on a rug. Before she asked him about the prayers—he figured she would—Michael laid out his view.

"I've got my doubts if God exists or not. But if he does, I wouldn't allow for certain things to happen."

She preferred not to doubt His existence. It was one of the determinations she'd made before the Wall.

They took the road that led to the Masada Fortress, and without stopping, they entered the primitive Highway

90, which bordered the Dead Sea and its moon-like landscape.

"We are at the lowest point on Earth. From here on, one can only go upward."

Aline had the feeling that she was leaving behind a world that had helped her see her future in a different light.

That night in Beit Hakerem, Michael did not return late from *The Post*, determined to face an unexpected reality that had taken hold of him.

Aline, with her thoughts still anchored in Beersheba, was bustling around the kitchen in jeans and a T-shirt, preparing dinner. The night in the desert had caused havoc in the very depth of her soul, and it took her hours to recover. Fate, gone haywire, placed the man who had just crossed the threshold in her path and who now, without beating around the bush, would speak to her bluntly. She knew beforehand that this was going to happen, but she was caught off guard when he revealed his feelings in such a forceful, deep, and sudden manner.

Michael took her hands in his with the determination of a man who knows what he wants. Then he spoke calmly.

"I've never felt for any woman what I feel for you. These feelings are out of my control. I'm aware of the difficulties that a relationship like ours would entail, in which I will not abandon my country and neither you nor your acquired commitments." Then, without taking his eyes away from hers, he added, "This isn't just a wish. It's something more, something unknown to me until now."

Aline stood leaning against the kitchen counter, listening to him. She, too, felt the urge to take a risk. And in a split second of lucidity, she thought that that restlessness and lack of control which had so often defined her life was once again before her, but this time around, to put things in order.

With this hope, as Michael kissed her neck, she whispered, "I'm willing to take the risk." And for a long while, she bathed in a flood of forgotten feelings.

Later, in the room, she felt the sweetness and a chemistry that she'd never been able to share with her husband. Michael's endless caresses had nothing to do with Partana's hurried ways, and she had never before experienced the passion discovered then. They made love all night long, as if it were the last time they'd be together…

"I don't want to lose you," Aline confessed, glued to his body at dawn.

"I'll be back in four days. Think no more."

He kissed her again before she disappeared down the stairs to make coffee, and he convinced himself that life offered opportunities even in the toughest times, but also that a woman like Aline wouldn't fall from the sky a second time. With these thoughts, he went to the bathroom and got into the shower.

In the room's jumble, as he was packing, he came upon Aline's passport. Her married name on that document was not unknown to him.

Shortly thereafter, as they stood hastily having their coffee in the kitchen, where last night's dinner was still half-cooked, Michael promised that he would join his father at his home in Rome the moment his busy schedule permitted. Aline only managed to say, "Give him a big hug."

The taxi driver's honking outside the door confirmed to the two of them that from then on, only the present mattered.

When Michael arrived at Ben Gurion airport, he went straight to check-in and was immediately escorted by a flight attendant to an office where a police officer checked his accreditation. At the foot of the runway, a van awaited. He was the last to enter the plane under the suspicious glances of the crew and the minister's security agents. The khamsin wind blew lightly.

CHAPTER 10

JERUSALEM, JULY 5, 1974

Aline snuggled into the large bed where she had made love with absorbing passion and tenderness. She couldn't help but think about how decisions put life at stake. That is what had happened with Partana; she'd changed hers. It was only a brief moment. Had she only turned down his marriage proposal on that night full of doubts, everything would've been different. Michael's "think no more" was infinitely more realistic than Partana's hasty decision in the Saudade. She was attracted to Guido's son's passionate character, which, together with his culture and physique, made him tempting.

Since her arrival at Schiller Street, Aline had made it a habit to stay up reading the texts of the book that Michael was writing till he got home at night. The laboriousness of those lines was a clear sign of his professionalism. All these traits not only did not leave her indifferent but permeated her entire being. An accumulation of sensations that sprung from the very bottom of her soul, all the way to living a new reality, had turned her into a more self-assured woman. Sorrow was fast lifting its heavy veil, and serenity began to prevail.

Yael was on a survival course in the Sinai desert, so Aline made plans without her. Michael gave her the phone number of some trusted friends, but she preferred to do her own thing. All that he told her before leaving was that she should do whatever she thought fit; he knew that she was capable of coping in the country on her own. She had proven it to him during the previous days and in the desert. It was hard to keep up with him, and she had done so during their trek across the Negev.

The old city captivated Henry's daughter, and as if drawn toward it like a magnet, she felt compelled to repeat her previous experience. She put on a pair of pants, a blouse, and comfortable sports shoes that would allow her to walk for hours. When she got into the taxi, she didn't notice the two individuals who, inside an old Citroën, didn't lose sight of her. Neither did she do so when she crossed the crowded Lions' Gate.

Engrossed and still feeling Michael's caresses on her skin, she made her way through the dirty and irregular laid-out cobbled streets of the Muslim Quarter. In a family restaurant, on one of the rooftops overlooking the Dome of the Rock, she had a light meal, whilst enjoying the breath-taking, magical views. She was eager to take in every single image. The distant chimes, mixed with the prayers of the muezzins, confounded her whilst forcing her to reflect. Aline believed herself to be living another millennium.

Afterward, she descended into the clutter of streets crammed with souvenir shops and street stalls selling fresh food. The people, a hotchpotch of races, mingled with each other like scents while merchants tried to lure tourists into their establishments. Aline got lost in the narrow, noisy, and colorful arched alleys that exuded the characteristic oriental atmosphere.

The two Turkish brothers hired by Bürke had been watching her for several hours, waiting for the right moment, which came when she crossed the threshold of Omar Manzur's three-story bazaar. One of them pretended to be interested in the stacked rugs, keeping an eye on Aline, who was wandering through the bazaar in a dim light among visitors, bags, and other odds and ends.

Omar was a stocky, elderly Arab who wore a white robe and had eyes as dark as they were expressionless. His dealings with the Turks had been frequent in recent months. They provided him with the hashish that, judging by the quantities he requested, must've made him a handsome profit on reselling it. Inside the room, behind the curtains where he did his accounts and charged his clients, the deal had been sealed: Aline would no longer be a problem. Manzur counted the bills. Although there were many, for a moment, he was suspicious. He immediately realized that if he didn't accept, they would quit selling him drugs. A refusal might even lead to worse consequences. He took it calmly as another part of the job.

It wasn't long before he was assisting her, which would allow him to execute the agreement that he'd made with the two brothers. She'd taken a fancy to a brass tray and was haggling over the price. When she was satisfied, Omar offered her an exquisite mint tea.

"It drives away fatigue at the end of the day," he said, handing her the cup.

Sitting in the small room, Aline didn't hesitate to drink it. Almost instantly, her vision clouded over, and in little less than a couple of minutes, the drowsiness prevented her from keeping her eyes open. It was the last sensation she experienced before falling completely asleep under the effects of the opium mixed with the infusion.

The Turks took her out wrapped in a *kilim* through the back door. She ended up at the bottom of the four-wheeled wooden cart that, at night, full of rubble and gear, Omar pulled. No one ever paid any attention to him or to the carts passing through the Lions' Gate at sunset. When Aline did so, hidden in the cart, the sun was setting, and the walls of Jerusalem took on a golden glow.

The Citröen was parked behind the house that was part of the Muslim cemetery at the end of Derech Sha'ar Ha Arayot Street. In a quick action, they transferred Aline's body to the trunk of the old vehicle.

The heat subsided. They left the necropolis and drove to Sultan Suleiman Street. From there, they took Highway 60. The khamsin wind was blowing. Even though night was falling, the sensation of fog, unalterable, would complicate the driving. Leaving Wadi Qelt to their right, they drove across the arid, mountainous area to Nablus, the city built with stones from Hebron in the valley between Mounts Ebal and Gerizim. The awful state of the road and the hateful wind forced them to slow down and get out of the car to make sure the woman in the trunk was still asleep.

The poor visibility further reduced their speed, but at the same time, it hid them. Nothing could be seen more than twenty meters away. The Turks expected to find the Israeli patrols on the border, some twenty kilometers south of Beit She'an, but they knew the terrain inside out, even where there were mines, and knew how to circumvent their surveillance. They were an hour away from the Jordanian border.

The Mossad operative had been trained to memorize. Every morning before leaving for work, he would review the files with the photos of the people that the secret service wanted to locate and have under surveillance. That week he was tasked with scouring the old city, posing as a traveling spice vendor. He immediately recognized, without the slightest doubt, the elegant, European-looking woman with dark hair and slanted eyes as she entered Manzur's store. He waited a long time for her to come out, but she didn't. Although she was not a relevant person, the Mossad wanted to know her moves within the country. Having lost track of the girl, he notified headquarters. His superiors had proof that the woman had given vital information unbeknownst to her and traveled to Israel for family reasons. Haim Weiss had made it very clear.

After 10:00 PM, the Citroën crossed a ford on the Jordan River, successfully dodging the obstacles. On the other side, in a desert setting, they saw the glow of lights coming from the vehicle of the German mercenaries, seasoned in the Second World War, who worked for Bürke and had contacts on the Jordanian side. Their insatiable warlike and commercial instinct meant that they were always in the midst of arms trafficking, corruption, and money. With a military appearance and fifty years under their belts, they were intimidating. The Turks approached them. They exchanged a few words before opening the trunk for them to retrieve Aline, still drugged. The well-built mercenaries unwrapped her from the *kilim* and stretched her out on the backseat of the Range Rover, which immediately disappeared in the darkness.

They camped long before reaching Irbid, in the ruins of a Roman settlement surrounded by dunes, under the full moon's glow. For the next twenty-four hours, she was the priority. Although they were experienced, the instructions they had been given, "bring her to me in perfect condition," went against their rules in the event of Aline's rebellion, but they had no choice but to do the job as ordered.

BEIRUT AND SHAJARA TOWN, JULY 6, 1974

In that luxurious, adventurous, and endearing Beirut, the traditional Lebanese house in Ras Beirut with its Mediterranean architecture had always been in the Rahhal family. It consisted of two floors, high ceilings, marble floors, antique wooden doors, and old mosaic tiles. It was surrounded by a lovely garden, like all those of its neighbors: Merchants, doctors, lawyers, and high-ranking government employees.

It was noon when Massoud crossed the central hall and climbed the steps, leaning on the stair railing, to the office, which, like the rest of the house, was decorated with Deco furniture. Reserved, he spoke in pithy sentences almost intentionally, as if not wanting to reveal more than was strictly necessary. His Arabian features were well defined, and his olive skin was accompanied by an enigmatic smile and a long nose. At seventy, he had replaced Ahmed's father in his council and in his heart ever since the latter's death in that boundless desert.

With the task of finding out everything about Erik Bürke and Aline Partana accomplished, it was time to inform Ahmed about his findings. He had never lied to him and was not about to do so now, although the danger was real.

A latent concern overwhelmed him since he'd been summoned a few days earlier in Bhamdoun, at the summer house, where he'd been asked to get this information. He immediately realized the special interest Ahmed showed for the Italian woman, which, as far as he could see, had little to do with his way of thinking or his understanding of life. She would complicate matters. The situation was a powder keg, and, in spite of his experience, he was unable to close the circle of events.

Gathered in the study, they sat down next to each other, and Massoud filled him in on the money he had given his bodyguards to sound out those of his cousin Georges.

"You know how it is in this underworld. The deeper you dive and pay, the more evidence you collect. That's how I found out about Bürke's threats to Aline, but no one can tell the reason for this brutal behavior. As a matter of fact, he was looking for Partana, but the latter was already dead."

Ahmed listened without the least trace of doubt on his countenance but with vengeance written across it, and Massoud found himself unable to prevent the inevitable. Giving him the information was as good as pushing him into a devastating void. Nonetheless, he carried on, "What I can guarantee is that the Norseman had a shipment intercepted that was destined for Georges. Trucks and men were blown up. He is beside himself, convinced that Aline works for someone and that he was set up. Neither do I understand how he's reached that conclusion, as much as I've racked my brain. The truth of the matter is that yesterday Aline Partana was in Jerusalem, and some Turks have orders to get her out of the country, but her whereabouts and Erik's intentions regarding her are a mystery."

Ahmed's inscrutable features gave no hint of the consternation that those disclosures had caused him. As he suspected, Aline's fear of Bürke had nothing to do with the proposition that he, without knowing who she was, had made to her in Ibiza through Erik.

He listened unflinchingly to the forceful words of his interlocutor echoing in the room.

"The freighter Kyssos anchored in Tartus this morning with another freight for your cousin. Erik is crossing Syria, making sure the trucks reach their destination. Delivery is scheduled to take place tonight at 11:00 PM in Jordan, about fifteen kilometers from the Israeli border." And sensing what was going to happen, he suggested, "If you're planning to travel, take your bodyguard with you. He knows the route inside out. It's my duty to warn you that doing so is not devoid of risks."

"Think of it as an experience that I've never been through," Ahmed replied, convinced that he would.

"I can't stop you, but is that woman worth it?"

"Find out for yourself, and you'll know…Where's Georges?" he asked, eager to change the conversation.

"In the casino, in the baccarat room. He always gives proof of his high income so that he is allowed to play, and when he concentrates on the cards, it's best to ignore him; although in this case, it's better this way," he said, thinking of the growing rift between the cousins. Ahmed did not approve of Georges' vices at the roulette or his illegal arms deals.

With a heavy heart, Massoud withdrew, leaving Rahhal to his thoughts but trusting in predestination, of which only the Arabs are capable. He hoped that fate wouldn't turn against Rahhal, although the latter always had an ace up his sleeve and never ceased to surprise him before adversity.

Once he reached the garden, he looked up and saw him through the window talking on the phone. He hadn't the slightest idea as to where to start, but the message was clear: Find out who Aline was. Undoubtedly, Ahmed had substituted interest for passion; he knew him too well to know that this was so. He had always paid for his relationships; he simply didn't care to mix sex and feelings. Ahmed was not in the habit of crossing deserts, risking his life for any woman.

The driver was cleaning one of the cars. He recognized the scent of oriental thyme. No doubt they were cooking *Manouche*, his favorite dish. He looked up again; Ahmed was still on the phone. Suddenly, something troubled him.

The desert had always been present in the life of the Rahhal family. For better and for worse. Massoud prayed.

Bürke knew that Aline would end up in his clutches, which would guarantee the success of his enterprise. He'd finally find out once and for all to whom she was passing the information on, and no one would dare intercept the cargo with her in his possession. He never had any scruples, least of all when zealously planning the operation to capture her. Convinced that his plans were the right ones, he turned all his attention to the journey and achieving his goals. He was accustomed to traveling in hellish terrain amid inhospitable climates and putting his life on the line, just like Georges did in the casinos.

He followed the three 4,5-tonne Leyland trucks heading for the Jordanian border from a safe distance in his black Range Rover. Two of the trucks were full of weapons and ammunition, the third of water and gasoline, and in each, two Turkish drivers were armed with Browning pistols. The port of Tartus had been left behind five hours earlier, and they were now driving along secondary roads, with the Qalamun mountain range to their left and the Anti-Lebanon mountain range, thick with Syrian pine and oak forests, to their right. The heat intensified as they approached the border along the narrow roads where hollows, valleys, and ravines opened up along the mountains. It was difficult to move at more than thirty kilometers per hour. Erik noticed that a slight khamsin blurred the horizon.

Aline woke up with a headache and a sour taste in her mouth. A strange heaviness prevented her from moving normally, as if she'd lost control over her body. She looked around; she was stretched out on a mattress inside an old, dilapidated house, or at least that is what she seemed to make out. She was terrified, unable to come to terms with what had happened. All she could remember was the tea she drank at the bazaar, and after that, nothing else.

It was a long time before she was able to clear her head with the water and food that had been left on the floor. When she finally managed to go outside, stiff and disoriented, she was blinded by the light. The hours that passed while she was unconscious had made her lose track of time. Surrounded by average-high rocky mountains, by steppe vegetation, and not a single tree on the horizon, she was overcome by the same feeling of solitude and silence that had struck her in the Negev desert, although Michael had been there and no one had deprived her of her freedom.

The possibility of escaping from such a peculiar place was impossible. Two burly men who looked like combatants, sitting inside a large Jeep, kept a close eye on her. She was unaware of their identity and their objective. She desperately sought their attention, eager for answers, but neither her screams nor her threats provoked a mere blink. One of them suggested in English that she rest. They'd be moving as soon night fell. Incredulous, Aline assumed that they would not yield and that the mystery of her situation would remain till she left that rough and abrupt hillock.

A subtle wind made her desist, and she stepped back into the settlement. She plucked her courage and figured that if she was still alive, it was because they needed something from her. She would not allow her discouragement to befuddle her and prayed to God, the same her father had turned to, the same Haim entrusted himself to in the synagogue and to whom Ahmed predicted that everything was in His hands. No doubt, one and the same. She asked Him that something unexpected occur and so be able to return to Beit Hakerem unscathed.

"Let no one tell someone who has already decided what their destiny is what he must do." That Arabic proverb applied one hundred percent to Ahmed's behavior on learning of the unforeseeable event and Erik's machinations regarding Aline. His instinct compelled him, convinced that face to face with the Norseman, he would find out where she was being held. The revenge he had planned, cold, thorough, and inexorable, rode alongside him.

They took off from Rue Bliss at five in the afternoon and drove past the American University, skirting the west coast along General de Gaulle Street till the racetrack. Nothing mattered faced with the anxiety of knowing that the only woman that he cared for was in serious danger.

As they made their way out of Beirut, it wasn't long before the Beqaa Region emerged as an oasis in the midst of the desert, at the bottom of two arid slopes of Anti-Lebanon. In its fertile red earth, vineyards, cereals, and sunflowers grew in abundance. From Chtaura to Masnaa, the Lebanese border with Syria, the distance was short. To Rahhal, it seemed eternal. They continued all the way to Daraa.

Bürke and his trucks, although further ahead, would have to avoid the border post, travel along narrow roads, cross the Yarmouk River Valley, and continue ten kilometers along the Shallallah River basin, which was dry at this time of year. His target was near Al-Shajara. Ahmed could avoid that itinerary, officially cross over to Jordan from Ar-Ramtha and position himself in the barren mountain steppe. Only the Syrian who was driving next to him knew the twists and turns to reach the exact spot. Mount Hermon, in all its splendor, full of beauty and poetry, accompanied them for much of the journey until night fell, and they disappeared behind it.

Rahhal meditated under the full moon, marred by the wind that rang like a loud whisper across those rocky promontories. He knew the Norseman's personality well enough to realize that, under pressure, he was capable of irrational acts, and this one bore Yurchenko's signature. The primary goal of the two Turks was abducting Aline and getting her out of Israel; for him, it was to locate Bürke and find out why he was acting so savagely in regards to Aline. But above all, to find her.

Ahmed's driver and bodyguard warned him that they wouldn't spot the trucks until they practically ran into them, for they were equipped with special lights that only lit up the roads in short distances. Moreover, visibility was poor.

"Whatever it is you have to do," the bodyguard hurried him, "do so quickly. Georges' men will check the cargo and disappear as soon as Bürke gives the order to hand over the keys to the trucks. And there will be no trace of him either."

Ahmed hardly listened to him, absorbed in his thoughts. He still couldn't figure out Aline's trip to Jerusalem and under what state she'd be or where. He felt responsible for her for having desired her without delving into her identity on that ill-fated night in Ibiza aboard the Ishtar. The pitiless khamsin wind accompanied them.

Aline was still at the ruins of the Roman settlement, where the khamsin was still blowing. Mercenaries referred to it as the "invisible enemy" of armed conflicts; in the Arab world, it was feared because it altered the body and irritated people's state of mind. It was a phenomenon that disrupted everything in its path.

Aline was not surprised when at dusk, one of the men made an appearance in that enclosure, whose walls had witnessed endless battles, and unceremoniously ordered her to follow him. With the dread in her body, she obeyed and concluded that it was time to find out who her abductor was and why. Her heart was pounding as she climbed into the Range Rover in that hell. Only Michael's strength, his knowledge and experience in extreme situations, came to mind. She saw him as the only person capable of getting her out of there.

That place's silence was crushing, as was that of the men who guarded her. She was unable to tell for how long the vehicle drove through the difficult desert roads, far from civilization, while she shuffled infinite possibilities as to why she was there without finding an answer.

Suddenly they stopped, and everything happened very quickly. The mercenaries ordered her out of the Range Rover. On doing so, Aline found herself on a plain battered by gusts of sand, making it impossible to see clearly. She couldn't make out anything more than a few meters away. The men dragged her to some dunes out of the wind's way and disappeared, or at least they were no longer near, for she could no longer see them. However, she did manage to catch a glimpse of a corpulent figure in the mist. She knew it was Bürke. He advanced aggressively, imbued with his characteristic vigor, that same vigor that put the fear of God into his competitors and herself. She recalled the words of the Lawyer Sassari at Villa Balbini, "Don't worry, Bürke won't bother you." Coming from him, there was no reason for it not to be so. If something had changed and the merchandise hadn't been delivered, then that left her defenseless. She began to shake.

Bürke knew that it was time to get even. He was short on time, and patience was not his forte. In his cogitation, he'd contemplated the risk of kidnapping her, but the urgency of knowing who she was working for outweighed all other considerations, even the threats from the Partana family. At the time, he'd gotten the merchandise, but not till Aline had been found alive. Now other businesses at stake put his life and hers at risk. Yurchenko would kill him in the blink of an eye if he didn't find out whoever it was that destroyed the last delivery destined for Georges. Bürke was sure that Aline was an important link in the events that had occurred a few days earlier.

His men and the trucks were only a few yards away. Invisible in the midst of the sandstorm, they awaited his orders. The minutes at his disposal were numbered, so he spoke with all the anger he was capable of.

"I didn't have you brought all the way here because of our last meeting at your apartment."

Aline wondered to herself, if "that" business had been resolved, what on earth had prompted Bürke to have some mercenaries kidnap her. In her confusion, she remained silent, waiting for what he'd say next.

"I want to know who you work for, and I want to know now." And just as he was saying this, he drew the Colt .45 that was sticking out of his shirt and, with the dust whipping around him and a few dunes as their only witnesses, aimed it at Aline.

A few minutes before this happened, Ahmed was on the last leg of his journey. It was getting dark, and the stars were conspicuous by their absence. He evoked the moments when, after his father died, he'd contemplate them from the infinite desert, searching for his father in them. The same thing that Aline used to do and that she confessed to him leaning on the balustrade of the Ishtar in Ibiza. He longed for the twinkling of tiny stars in the sky on this dark, dusty, and windy night at a close distance from Shajara Town.

He knew he had to be quick. When it came to arms deliveries, people were always on edge, and time was of the essence. Following his intuition and, taking into account that Bürke's previous delivery had been foiled, nothing at this stage could be ruled out.

His bodyguard, on the other hand, could hardly understand why a man of Rahhal's rank had picked this fight. He realized that everything had been decided in advance and that some powerful force pushed him forward, not wanting to see the danger that lay ahead. He shook those thoughts from his mind and, based on his experience, warned his boss that the sandstorm was subsiding. This would make it easier to make out the esplanade and reach the hillock. It was as clear as daylight that every minute was of the essence, so much so that there was no need to articulate it.

On reaching the hillock, Ahmed grabbed the binoculars and carefully scanned the terrain. He spotted the trucks and the men that Bürke had paid to make the delivery, and some others, Georges', to take charge of the consignment. Suddenly, the Norseman's silhouette, blurred and a few yards from the rest of the entourage, became visible. He was walking toward his black Range Rover, parked near the dune. He opened the door, got into the vehicle, and sat down as if he was waiting for some reason to move ahead with the business at hand. What was holding Bürke back from handing over the keys to the trucks and disappearing from this hell of a place? Ahmed felt that something was not quite right.

"Is there any way to get to him without the men intercepting us?" He asked his bodyguard, handing him the binoculars. The latter grabbed them and skimmed the horizon. He knew the area inside out. Before answering him, he weighed the chances of success or failure, although it was clear to him that Rahhal was going to bet everything on one card.

"There is a parallel path, but if they locate us without knowing our identity, they could shoot us. The last section can be done on foot. It's only a few meters."

"We must seize this moment. I want to reach him where he is now, away from his people and the trucks," Ahmed replied with resolve. Then, as he was in the habit of doing, he murmured, "May Allah protect us."

The escort, on hearing these words, had no need for further questions. He accelerated and headed for the agreed-upon place.

The minutes seemed endless. The moon moved slowly across the sky, hiding behind clouds at intervals, casting everything in darkness. When this happened, the threat of being discovered by the men on the esplanade diminished, and they advanced more boldly. They did so until the start of the rocky terrain that swooped down toward Bürke's Range Rover.

"Watch my back," Ahmed ordered, aware that the Nordsman's violence would increase if he showed up with his armed escort. "I will descend the slope alone."

And without another word, he darted down, but what he never imagined was that he'd find Bürke at the edge of the dune taking aim at Aline under a leaden sky.

Both their faces contorted when they saw the Lebanese appear. Ahmed immediately realized that an uncontrolled action on his part would prompt Bürke to shoot, regardless of his presence. The outcome could be tragic.

The man before him did not resemble the one who used to sail aboard the Ishtar, the one who dined surrounded by beautiful women and pretended to be a respectable businessman. Bürke now showed his true face, the one he showed when his transactions went awry, that of the impulsive and ruthless man.

Ahmed noticed the weariness and tension on Aline's face. He immediately asked if she was okay, trying hard not to show his concern and feigning an authority that he lacked in the present circumstances. She nodded, but inside was petrified with fear, unable to figure out what was going on. In her bewilderment, she sensed that Ahmed was on her side. Bürke, without letting go of the weapon, questioned him and asked how he had found him.

"Massoud obtained information on your movements."

Bürke knew very well who Rachid Massoud was and how he acted. But in this situation, it was not what worried him the most. Having a witness to the events like Rahhal complicated matters. He needed to give the orders for the truck drivers to get moving; he had delayed it because he wanted to question Aline before they took off. Perhaps the mole linked to her was right there. Rahhal's question was immediate.

"What do you want from Aline?" He asked, assuming that at this point, he wouldn't lie to him.

"Your friend here took a document from Georges' briefcase the afternoon she was with you in Nice aboard the Sapphire. I'm eager to find out who she works for and to whom she passed the information. It's the key to finding out who sabotaged my penultimate deal."

Cornered, Aline felt a cold shudder run down her spine on recalling Haim translating the paper in the small restaurant in the Trastevere district of Rome. He led her to believe that it had to do with the purchase of a new yacht for Marco. He lied to her. But why? What was Haim hiding? And how come he was able to sabotage Bürke's shipment? She found it hard to believe. What's more, she couldn't even imagine it. And since she wasn't sure why, she wasn't going to name him. Haim was her friend, her confidante, her supporter. She would never betray him.

She knowingly lied under Ahmed's impassive gaze.

"I took that paper because Marco Partana's name was on it, but afterward realized that they were written in Arabic, and I don't speak that language. So, I reconsidered. If, when married to Marco, I didn't know about his business affairs, why, dead, would I care to know?"

She thought that Bürke would pull the trigger at her words, but he didn't.

The Norseman collapsed under volleys of gunfire. It was impossible to figure out where they were coming from. Ahmed lunged at her, protecting her with his body as he pushed her into a ditch for cover. The confusion was total, and the shooting didn't stop. From the deep hole where they were sheltered could be heard the noise of the explosions, and all that could be seen were the flashes of the violent bursts.

Aline noticed that Ahmed's shirt was soaked with blood. She tore it open and saw that a bullet had pierced his back. Crouching beside him, she rested his head on her lap. Dismayed and with no one to ask for help, she realized that the injury was serious. The question had to be asked now or never.

"Why have you come all the way here to defend me?"

"I was indebted to you. You saved my nephew Ali in Paris from being crushed to death under the wheels of a car. You risked your life. That afternoon in Nice, when I saw your amulet, I asked you who'd given it to you. You told me the story, the same one my sister had told me years earlier. Ali is like a son to me," he said with a faltering voice; he had difficulty talking.

She remembered the kid with the floppy ears and thought that, when one least expects it, one returns to the starting point. Those were the days when she was struggling to hold on to the farmhouse when the trip to the Upper Ampurdán had become the beginning of a new existence that had propelled her so far from the old farmhouse, all the way to that desert where Ahmed was now dying to repay her action.

Aline didn't know what to say. Tears ran down her cheeks. Ahmed found the strength to speak,

"What did you do with the paper? It seems everything has happened because of it…"

"I showed it to a friend of mine who knows Arabic, and then we got rid of it. I never found out its true content."

"Is your friend Jewish?"

"Yes."

"Don't look for the why, Aline."

Ahmed realized that Aline's intimate friend had something to do with the first aborted delivery. He would've sworn that he worked for the Israeli government, but he suspected that she'd never know the truth.

The stars began to appear one by one in the sky. Ahmed, slowly, as if he were talking to them, spoke his last words, "It may be the Night of Destiny," he choked. "Pray and make a wish."

When she thought that despair would do her in, with Ahmed dying in her arms, someone approached her and, with unusual strength and solemnity, said, "I'm Lieutenant Hari Stern from the Israeli border patrol." He avoided telling her that he was part of the Mossad special forces. "Calm down. Everything is under control."

He leaned down to see the wound. "Irreversible," he thought to himself. The bullet had undoubtedly lodged in his lung. Ahmed expired.

"We'll take care of him," Stern shouted, for the noise of the helicopter's engine, a few meters from them, forced him to do so. "Come with me," he said resolutely, seeing her powerless, with the Lebanese's body on her lap, as if she couldn't believe what had happened. "We'll take you to a field hospital."

Aline had difficulty standing up; a mere exhalation would have knocked her down. When she finally managed to do so, she saw a significant deployment of soldiers and armored vehicles on the plain.

The lieutenant helped her into the helicopter. He immediately gave orders: To her, to breathe deep; to the pilot, to take off. When they ventured forth into the dark gray sky, with the moon that seemed to be chasing them, Aline remembered Ahmed in Ibiza, when he told her that the Arabs were taught to be prepared for their death and that of their loved ones, stressing that she too must learn to do so, and accept her father's. At the time, she thought it was an impossibility, as impossible as that a man with whom she had had only two conversations, conceive the idea of coming out to the desert to save her because of a moral debt that he considered pending.

The half-tracks, covered in camouflage netting, had remained hidden while a score of soldiers armed with Uzi submachine guns crawled on the ground led by Lieutenant Stern. With meticulous professionalism, they finished off the traffickers in a matter of minutes. Now, as Aline and the lieutenant flew back to camp, his men would seize the truckloads of weapons and take prints from the bodies to analyze at headquarters. They would perform an autopsy on Ahmed Rahhal's body to find out which side the projectile that killed him belonged to.

The wind was no longer blowing, and the darkness had lifted.

JERUSALEM, JULY 7, 1974

Intelligence Officer Yadin Tag entered one of the white tents that had a cross on the roof and which were located next to a flat field that served as landing pads for the helicopters. The tents housed the operating rooms where the seriously wounded were treated immediately, as well as for the kidnapped victims, who, according to protocol, had to spend a few hours there to be debriefed. His superior had informed him about the kidnapping of Aline Asher and also about the information that, unbeknownst to her, she'd provided. Piecing together the hours before Lieutenant Stern's intervention was his business.

She'd never know that she was rescued thanks to Ahmed Rahhal. For years, the wealthy Lebanese had been passing information to the Mossad about high-ranking government officials in his country in exchange for economic concessions that benefited his business affairs. The reason why the previous day he had contacted one of his collaborators in Beirut informing him of the exact location in exchange for her protection continued to baffle him, all the more so when he learned that Rahhal had driven to where the clash had taken place, regardless of the danger involved.

Aline spent the night sedated but was now ready to have a cup of coffee and answer questions in the small bar in one of the tents. She did so thoroughly but, at the same time, as if her mind was processing a long tangle. She took it for granted that she had no choice.

After all, she was safe.

In the rebirth to reality, she couldn't stop thinking about Haim and what part he had played in those terrible events. The future conversation with her faithful companion would be long, despite the fact that Ahmed told her to forget about it.

The officer warned her that hostages always remained in a state of shock for a few days, if not more.

"You were lucky to have been abducted for only a few hours."

Aline didn't dare acknowledge the relief she felt knowing that Bürke's remains lay scattered in the desert.

Tag, having made the inquiries, arranged for a soldier to accompany her to the house on Schiller Street that appeared in the dossier, which stated that she'd spent the last few weeks with a renowned journalist, unconnected to the events.

Ahmed's body lay at the other end of the hospital. Tag went in search of the doctor who'd removed the bullet. When the latter put it on the table, he studied it. It wasn't one of theirs. Clearly, a stray bullet hit him during the fray. Rahhal was a good collaborator. His secret would become part of his blood, as the Arabs said. Now, dead, according to his beliefs, he'd wake up from the deep sleep that his life had been.

PARIS

Haim Weiss had gone to the family home in Paris to spend a few days. At sunset, he headed to the *Bois de Boulogne*. A long walk would help ease the stress he'd felt ever since he'd learned of the denouement in Shajara Town and the danger he'd put Aline through. The night they dined in Trastevere, he was unable to talk her out of her trip to Israel, just as it was his duty to inform his superiors of his discoveries and hide from her, as from everyone else, his true identity. Aline would most likely be on her way to her farmhouse. She'd need a good amount of time to recover from a situation like the one she'd just gone through.

The night before, his boss had informed him of Aline's kidnapping and of Bürke's decision to change the arms route. He explained that he'd received the information through a Lebanese collaborator with whom they'd reached an agreement to protect Aline in exchange for the information. As Haim walked surrounded by cedars, he thought that the deal the Lebanese had struck with his people was a part of the story still unknown to him. But he would investigate. It was his job.

Aline was like a magnet, which attracted dangerous situations. Now, after so many experiences, he hoped that she'd now realize that sometimes in life, there is no other option but to lie. Her years with the Partana family would make it easier for her to understand this.

He recalled their walks years ago, along the same paths he was on now; how he guided her in the same beliefs that Henry had instilled in her and that she followed after his death. Perhaps those principles gave Aline the strength to face what was to come. His contacts had now informed him of her relationship with a Jewish journalist. He would be her greatest support to forget what had happened.

He was a short distance away from the Lambert's house, from where he'd picked her up on so many occasions. Little did they imagine, back then, that they'd have to hide a part of their existence from that lovely family, which had taken such good care of her. Aline, her years with Partana and its consequences, and he, his double life. There were things that could not be explained on this earth, but the universe always colludes and gives one an answer.

He was engrossed in these thoughts when a young man with pointed ears crossed his path. His memory never failed: He was the Lebanese boy, a few years older, a neighbor of the Lamberts. It crossed his mind that perhaps he might have something to do with the Lebanese from Beirut.

He suddenly realized that it had been way too long since he'd last been to the synagogue. He directed his steps toward the one on the Rue de Tournelle, where he went with Aline whenever possible.

CHAPTER 11

UPPER AMPURDÁN, 1974

The soft fragrance of the pine trees greeted Aline as it always did when she returned to the farmhouse. However, this time around, the shots and the broken voice of Ahmed dying before her impotence still echoed in her ears.

Thinking about the hastily written note she left Michael as an excuse for her unexpected departure made her feel worse than she already did. She imagined his concern when no one answered his calls on Schiller Street. Michael didn't shy away from commitments, either on the job or in life, and she'd shied away from them, traumatized by the latest events. Violence and anguish of sudden deaths were nothing new to him, as he had captured in his articles during the Yom Kippur War, but she had had to face a hitherto ignored brutality.

Aline needed the reassurance of her surroundings and to figure out how she would explain to him why she ended up surrounded by mercenaries at an arm's drop. He would demand the truth of her. The decision was so difficult that she pushed open the door of the little stone house, sure that within its walls, she'd find the answer. She sat across from Henry's desk. She now understood more clearly his trip to Israel, the search for his roots, and why he used to tell her,

"To those which you must return to if you want to be happy."

The experiences in that country and finding Michael had been decisive in figuring out what was the best path to follow. She saw the branches of the fig tree through the window, and the Hebrew saying spoken by Guido came to mind: "You'll see which way the wind blows." Now she knew.

She turned her gaze at the shelves, where the photos of Henry, the grandparents, and hers were, and she suddenly realized that Patricia's was missing there. She opened one of the drawers. Her father's letter was where she had left it. Calmly, she reread his advice and his last wish: That Pat visit the farmhouse and that together they chat in front of the fireplace. She'd have her father's last wish come true as soon as possible.

The dogs' barking prompted her to step outside. José the Fisherman walked behind them rather slowly. The two of them merged into a hug that captured unexpressed feelings on his part.

"Will you come down to the tavern?"

"Not today. The trip has been a long one."

"I can imagine…But I'll be waiting for you tomorrow. Do you still remember how to sing habaneras?"

Aline confirmed this as she petted the puppies. He went back to his chores, and she went up to her room. She longed for Michael's strength, the passion and pleasure she felt while making love to him, and the sunsets in Beit Hakerem.

RAS BEIRUT

An envoy from the business office of the Israeli government had just left the house on Rue Bliss after presenting his condolences and handing Rachid Massoud an envelope containing the paperwork to take charge of Ahmed Rahhal's corpse. His body, in a zinc box covered with wood and welded on the outside, was traveling to Beirut via Cyprus. Given the non-existent relations with Israel, there was no other option but this one. Massoud, with a face ashen with grief before the inexplicable scenario, wandered through the same room where he had warned Rahhal not to make that trip. No one except him was aware of the loss of the man who held the reins and ran the family business.

He prayed, listening to the relatives' bustle on the ground floor, going about their day-to-day life in that suffocating month of July, oblivious of the misfortune that had befallen them. As it was written in their culture, upon death, one always leaves some unfinished business because one never knows when it shall befall. Ahmed left too many things unfinished, and he sensed that a good many others, in due time, would come to light.

He had sent for Georges, who was still in the casino north of town. The wait was devastating. He would have been hard put to say how long it took before he burst into the room. The prayers were long. When he gave him the news, Georges did not believe what had happened until he read the documentation. He collapsed. Rachid's immediate task was to make him swear, despite the painful moment, that Aline Asher's presence at the delivery would never come to light. Avoiding revealing how he found out about her, he told him about the kidnapping ordered by Bürke and why Ahmed went to Jordan. Georges gave him a disturbed look and shared with him the Norseman's suspicions aboard the Sapphire. That "I'll look into" that now weighed like a slab.

"There is more; I'll tell you who it is. Ahmed knew her identity. I didn't. But I informed myself."

And Massoud told him in a solemn tone how his cousin Ali's life was saved, to the stupor of the young Lebanese, who had never suffered incidents of such magnitude in his flesh.

"They're all dead," he continued cautiously. "Yurchenko has no evidence that proves Aline Asher's presence at the skirmishes. Neither you nor I know if she works for the Mossad." Then, strengthening his chin and with the attitude of one who has assumed the fatality, he declared, "Our commitment to her is infinite."

For a split second, it appeared as if Georges were putting two and two together on his own. He asked if his cousin had gone to Jordan just to pay off the debt or if there was something more.

"That's why he did it. Before leaving," Massoud said, "these were his words: 'She's a woman with whom you could cross the Nile.' That's how he defined her."

Georges reached his own conclusions. Bürke was unable to prove his suspicions. Inevitably, the ball was in Yurchenko's court. Nothing could be proved, and the only thing that was real was what happened in Rue Poussin; of that, he was sure, as sure as when the poker of aces was in his hand. He then swore that his secrets would be safe with him.

Loyal Rachid had other secrets to keep. Aline came from a Jewish family and had been Ahmed Rahhal's great love.

SICILY

Luca found out about Bürke's bullet-riddled death in the Middle East just when his father, Don Giovanni, had given the go-ahead to get rid of him. No one knew who was behind the Norseman's death, but whoever it was had saved them of an inevitable job.

Luca had always hated Bürke because he considered him a dishonest and treacherous fellow, and above all, because, if he had not crossed Marco's life, everything would be different. He still hadn't gotten over the loss of his brother; the feeling that something fundamental was missing in his life was constant. Marco's loyalty, coupled with his gift for coordinating and contacting high-level people, made him irreplaceable.

That morning Luca had urgent affairs to deal with, but he put everything aside and, accompanied by his bodyguards, got into one of his cars and drove to his father's house in the Bologneta countryside in an oppressing heat. As he penetrated the countryside, the vegetation's fragrance made him recall his childhood with Marco in that landscape. Those memories haunted him till he reached his destination.

When he arrived at the villa, he spotted his father and Michele Sassari sitting on the terrace, in the shade of the trees, having a cold drink. They immediately sensed that if Luca showed up unannounced, there must've been a good reason. They hugged each other as was their wont, and the two men listened to his words, which were brief because little else was known about the Norseman's death.

Don Giovanni confessed that he was relieved to learn that Bürke was no longer in the world of the living and, moreover, that Marco's wishes had been fulfilled. He suddenly asked about Aline; ever since he'd given the order that she be protected, he hadn't uttered her name, overwhelmed by the pain of Marco's death and because Sassari had informed him that everything had been taken care of. And as if Michele had the answer to his question, he gave the latter a look that called for a precise answer.

Michele sought to convey serenity and replied, "She's smart and will keep her promises. I'm sure everything will be fine."

He kept to himself that on his way out of Villa Balbini, his intuition had told him that Aline, given her curiosity and courage, would not be free of further setbacks.

Don Giovanni, oblivious to the thoughts of his right-hand man, breathed calmly, unable even to imagine that Aline had witnessed Bürke's death. Only the Mossad knew about it, which left no trace of its operations; Ahmed Rahhal, who had died; and Massoud and Georges Haleemi, who would keep quiet forever because Ali was alive thanks to her.

Perhaps someday, Haim Weiss would manage to tie the story together. He was the only one who could do so.

UPPER AMPURDÁN

The twilight's golden light was fading, and nature seemed to abate as if, at the end of the day, all feelings were drained along with it. Aline, sitting on the edge of the pond, saw Michael at the end of the cypress-lined path, and she understood that he hadn't called because he wanted to clarify her flight face to face. She stood still. The path, always that path in the worst of times and in the happiest, too. Blissful when she covered it with her father, tragic when with Doris she left her childhood behind and anxiety-riddled with Partana. Now definitive.

Michael went straight to the point, as was always the case with him. Beating around the bush was not his style.

"I want to understand," he said, thinking that even if he hit it on the nail, she'd have to pour her heart out.

All he had to do was pronounce her last name, the one he saw in her passport, to his colleagues at the *Corriere della Sera* for them to bring him up to date on the Santacroces and Henry's daughter's ties to that family.

"I know that Marco Partana was your husband, and there is no need for you to clarify the past, but you didn't leave because of this."

Aline saw in him such determination that any comment on her part would have been superficial, and she didn't want to squander their relationship by lying to him. She asked him to follow her to the little stone house, feeling a sudden sense of serenity.

"Come, I have lots to tell you."

And she explained to him why matters of import needed to be discussed within its four walls.

Sitting on the worn-out leather sofa, a witness of so many dialogues of the Ashers, Michael listened to her. All that had happened to her had left profound impressions on her. He, who lived writing stories, considered that the one that Aline was relating to was overwhelming. He had a thousand questions for her, but she was in no condition to answer them. They agreed not to talk about that past anymore, ready to rescue the harmony of the last couple of weeks prior to her kidnapping.

Despite this, Aline's confident voice filled the room, "I will sign the contract with the Americans and spend two years on the other side of the Atlantic. It will be hard for me to live without you," she declared as something inevitable but thoroughly meditated.

Michael was not surprised. She had the right to be everything she wanted to be and go as far as her talents would allow her to, without interference. It was now up to him to make some resolutions if he didn't want to lose her. This meant either putting aside his current life or taking time out to finish his novel. Leaving Italy to work in Jerusalem had been a decision of the same magnitude, a leap into the void without a safety net.

"What do you think?" Aline asked.

"I'll tell you tomorrow." And with a spontaneity that must've had something to do with his inner turmoil, he continued, "I'll sleep here tonight if you don't mind." He pointed to the sofa. "This shelter is ideal for meditating."

"It's as he left it. I haven't moved a single piece of paper. His notes, his photos…"

Seeing that her father's absence still pained her, he suggested the perfect excuse to get her out of there.

"Come, show me the farmhouse and these oak forests that you described so well in the Negev." He stood up and, reassuringly, took her by the hand.

On closing the door, Aline suddenly spoke to him, "Michael, what is the Night of Destiny?"

"It's one of the last ten nights during Ramadan. For Muslims, the heavens part, and prayers and pleas go straight to God."

"Ahmed, in the throes of death, urged that I do so. I prayed in my own way."

"And did you ask for anything? That night is so special for them that if they listen to you in the afterlife, it can change your destiny."

"Yes, but I'll also tell you tomorrow."

It was that time of the evening when it is neither day nor night, that hour in which Aline was in the habit of going for a walk with Henry.

ACKNOWLEDGEMENTS

My deepest gratitude to **Eduardo Martín de Pozuelo**, a journalist who knows so much about the mafia, for his patience. To **Maya Mahler** for opening doors for me. To **Montserrat Martínez** for being the best guide in Israel and to **Alhan Charara**, who transmitted to me the beauty and her love for Beirut.

I cannot go without mentioning the Jewish communities of Barcelona and Madrid for their kindness and closeness.

To **Noah Klieger**, and my fond memory of him.